More Tales told
near a Crocodile

BY THE SAME AUTHOR

Tales told near a Crocodile

Black Samson

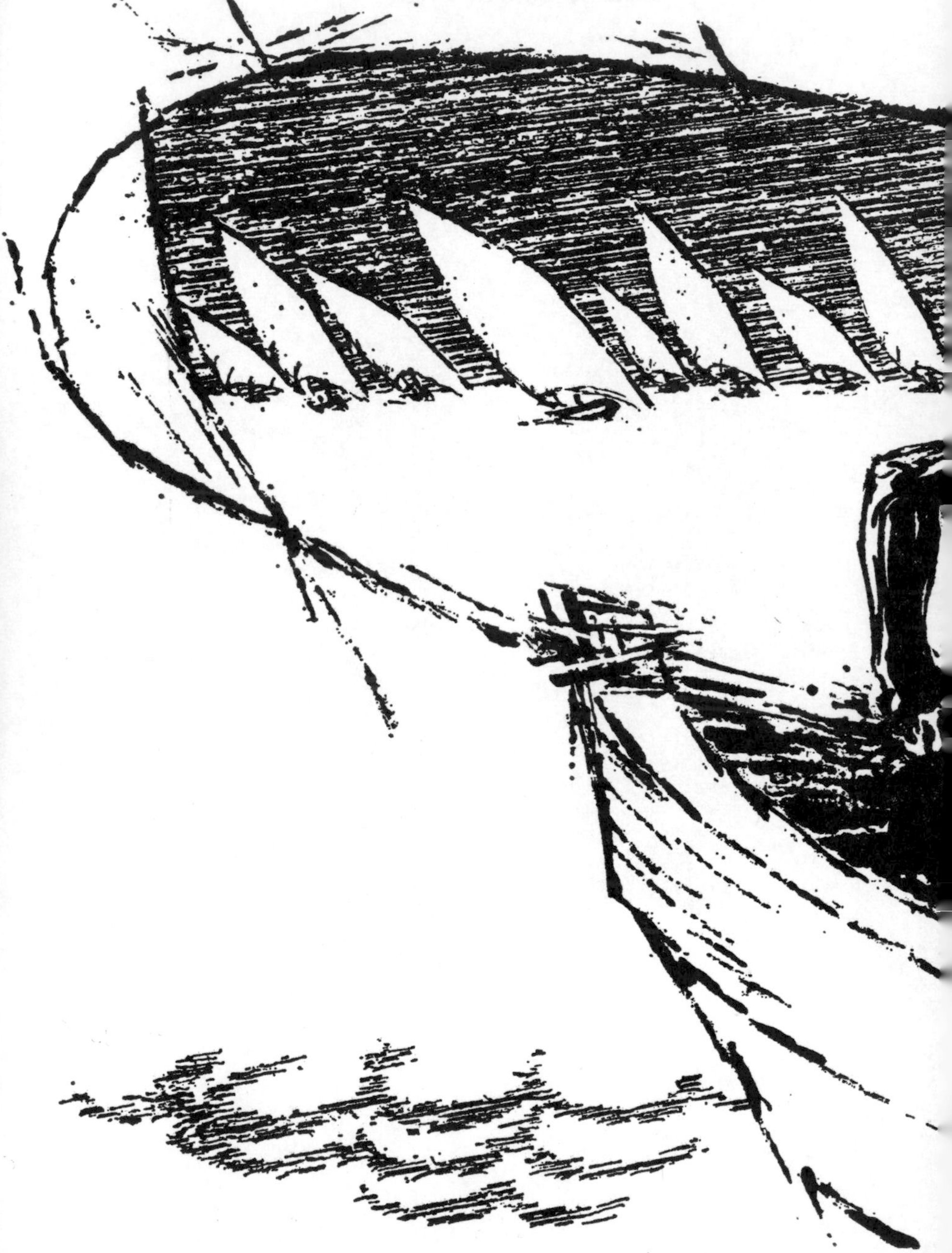

More Tales told near a Crocodile

HUMPHREY HARMAN

Illustrated by Beryl Sanders

HUTCHINSON OF LONDON

HUTCHINSON JUNIOR BOOKS LTD
3 Fitzroy Square, London W1

London Melbourne Sydney Auckland
Wellington Johannesburg Cape Town
and agencies throughout the world

First published 1973

ISBN 0 09 114390 X

This book is for
KAREN CLARE

Contents

Introduction   13

Dirobo   17

The Leopard   25

Libina the Coward   33

King Lion   47

Omolo and Sabala   53

Zebra   66

Kirui and Kipkelat   73

Kakara the Giver   83

The Hawk and the Hen   104

The Honey Bird   108

The word 'simi' is used in several of these stories. A simi is a kind of sword once used by a number of East African tribes, and it looks like this:

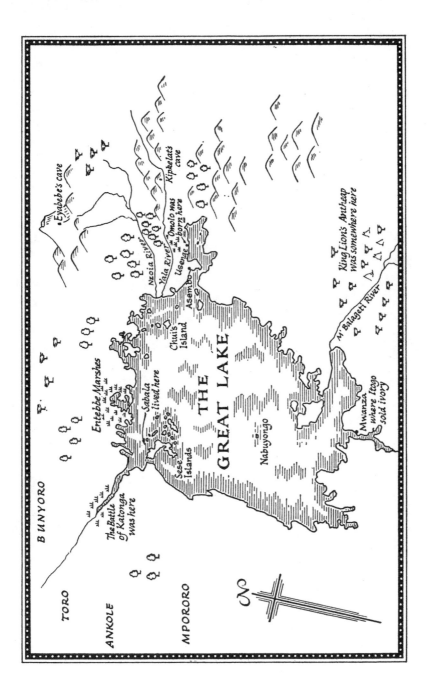

BUNYORO

TORO

ANKOLE

MPOROKO

Eyaebe's cave

Kipkelat's cave

Omoto was born here

Nzoia River

Yala River

Usenge

Asembo

Chui's Island

Entebbe Marshes

Sabala lived here

Sese Islands

The Battle of Katonga was here

Nabuyongo

THE GREAT LAKE

King Lion's Antheap was somewhere here

Mt Balagetti River

Mwanza where Itago sold ivory

N

Introduction

The Great Lake of these stories is Lake Victoria, that vast, fresh-water sea, deep inside the continent of Africa. An atlas shows that it is crossed by the Equator, and lies upon a plateau three thousand feet high; that its coasts enclose some sixty thousand square miles of water, and belong to three countries, Kenya, Tanzania, and Uganda. It also reveals that Victoria is one of the two sources of the River Nile.

Maps say as little about the flavour and mystery of places as time-tables tell of journeys. The precise line which is the lake coast may, in reality, be marshes many miles wide, deep buried in papyrus, and veined by tortuous creeks. No one there can say where land ends and water begins. The islands of the map are neatly limned, but not the floating islands of matted reeds, torn by storms from marshes, and sailing past with marooned snakes or even buck as unwilling passengers. The map is silent about schools of sleeping hippo or crocodile on sandbanks which quiver in the heat, about raucous parrots in waterside trees, or birds with names like ibis, hammerkop or whydah, and great saddle-billed storks with mouths like swords. There is nothing about storms which, in a minute, can whip the lake into angry chaos, and as quickly die, or eels that can bite a boot off a man, with the foot inside, and slender fishing boats beneath great three-cornered sails, with painted eyes on the bows to find the way home through darkness.

Or about people.

When an African talks of 'my people' only rarely does he mean what we mean. Words like Kenyan and Tanzanian are modern innovations, and still largely exist only in the mouths of politicians. 'My people' means my tribe, and the tribes living on the Great Lake's shores and islands, or in the surrounding forests and hills, can be counted by scores. They are as varied as the pieces of a jigsaw, nomadic warrior herdsmen, like the Masai, Samia fishermen, Luo peasant farmers, or forest hunters such as the rare Wadirobo. In the past these people managed to get along, rather in the manner of big families (which, indeed, sometimes they were), without presidents or policemen, mayors or magistrates, to tell them what to do. Many had not even invented the idea or office of chief. But in what is now Uganda there were tribes with kings and thrones, palaces and courts, provincial governors and armies.

One thing, however, they all possessed—a great fund of stories, and since reading and writing was unknown, they told them. The ten stories in this book were collected from eight of the tribes that live near the lake.

Two kinds of people told stories. Usually it was Grandmother. African women worked hard. Beside caring for children, cooking, brewing, pot-making, fetching water and making clothes, they grew the crops. A man's business was fighting, hunting, house-building, cattle-herding, and the ceremonial side of life. The rest he left to women. So, usually, Mother was far too busy for stories. It was Grandmother, her children off her hands, and work done, who told them to grandchildren, and from her that every child learnt the stories of his tribe.

The other story-teller was almost a professional, a gifted man who would amuse and instruct adults as well as children.

It is impossible to translate African stories to the printed page without losing almost every quality of the original. They were, and are, a form of art unknown to the West. There was one teller, but most of the audience would know the story, and not expect to merely sit and listen. They would take part, answer the teller's questions in chorus, grunt agreement or shout denial at appropriate places. Often the story would change abruptly into song, and the listeners had a part to sing. The teller might use drum or harp, and there might be dancing.

Words on paper cannot convey this. A paragraph summarising the story of ballet or opera omits everything of the original that counts. So does a written African story. All one can do is to take the event which lies at the heart of every one of them—and it may be the frailest cobweb of an incident—and on this build a story in the sense we understand it. That is as much as I have tried to do.

Chalimbana, 1973   H.H.

Dirobo

In the beginning they say that there was nothing except the earth. Rock and sand, crusted soil, lake and river, it stretched for ever, bald as an egg, and empty as a drum. And in the middle of this lived the god Asis, and his queen Sebeni.

The bare earth satisfied Asis, who liked life uncluttered, but Sebeni, who was very beautiful, wrinkled her nose, and made a small sad noise of discontent. 'It is all the same, and far too big,' she complained. 'There is nothing to capture the eye. I long for variety.'

Asis was concerned. 'I didn't know you were unhappy,' he said. 'What can I do?'

'Make things,' said Sebeni. 'Many, many things, and cover this emptiness.'

Asis hesitated. 'It is easy to make,' he said, 'but there is a small difficulty which it would be wise to consider now. There is a law which says that whatever is made must be lived with.'

'I'm quite sure,' said Sebeni, 'that anything my husband made would be perfect, and a pleasure to live with. Make things, Asis.'

'Very well,' said Asis, and he did. He made grass and trees. He made the small, weak plants that burst through iron soil to flower for a day, and the giant baobab that stands rooted for ever. He made gladioli to adorn the veldt, lilies at the water's edge, moss to crawl over rock, and the plants that gently wave in water. He made winds to move all these and rain to nourish them.

Sebeni walked through the new forests, and held out her hands for the pleasure of watching shadow and sunlight move on them. She plucked flowers, and plaited grass into rings. 'Clever, clever, Asis!' she cried, and laughed with delight. For a month. Then she grew discontented again.

'I was mistaken,' she said. 'This doesn't make me happy. It's fine, in a way, but you can only look at it. I want things that move and speak, see and hear. Make things that live as we do, Asis.'

He sighed. 'But . . . but . . . I must remind you,' he said, 'of that small rule. There can't be any second thoughts about what I make.'

'I believe,' replied Sebeni, and she smiled to soften the words, 'that you say these things in order to avoid trouble. You're lazy, Asis.'

'Very well,' he said, and made animals. For the veldt he made zebras, giraffes and lions, the jackals, hyenas and antelopes, and a host of other creatures. The forests he peopled with elephants and leopards. He gave the trees to monkeys and bush-babies, placed lizards on the rocks and scorpions beneath them. Among the reeds were pigs and buffaloes, and in the water crocodiles and catfish. Birds wheeled in the air, butterflies visited flowers, and the mole burrowed beneath the earth. Everything had its place.

Sebeni walked among the animals, and they raised their heads and spoke to her in their way. They allowed her hand to take pleasure in the softness of their wet black noses, or work in warm, rough fur. And when she bathed, shoals of tiny fish nibbled at her toes. She was happy beyond description. For a month.

Because there were now so many things on the earth, and their needs differed so greatly, Asis was away much of the time, seeing that all went well with what he had made. Sebeni complained about this.

'I'm lonely,' she sighed.

Asis was astonished. 'But you've all the animals I made,' he said.

'And they're interesting,' she replied, 'but they don't help my loneliness. It's true they speak, but I don't understand what they say. And they listen, but don't understand me. They live but they're strangers. Make something,

Asis, that thinks and believes, and speaks, and feels, and does as we do.'

At this Asis sat down beside his queen, and said slowly, 'It's possible to do this, but . . . but . . . think carefully, Sebeni. If I made a creature of this kind, and we grew to dislike it, still it must be lived with. What's made, cannot be unmade.'

'Do this one thing more for me, Asis,' cried Sebeni, 'and I will never ask you for anything more!'

'Very well,' said Asis, and that day he made Dirobo.

Dirobo is the oldest of men. He is small, strong, stocky, and the colour of honey. He has neat flat ears that can hear the lightest footfall, quick eyes that can see in the dark, and he follows scent like a leopard. He curls in grass to sleep, wants little, makes little, comes and goes like a shadow, and you do not see him unless he wishes you to.

Dirobo stood, all new, before Sebeni, and smiled secretively.

He was clever. Show him a thing done once and he could do it also. When Asis built a house, Dirobo watched, and then built another, precisely the same. But then he went back to his grass nest to sleep. When Sebeni made a pot, Dirobo took clay, and skilfully coiled just such another perfectly. And then he scooped water from the stream and drank from his hands. He hoed the planted ground exactly as he saw both of them do. But when the garden was finished he plucked wild fruit, and dug for roots to eat, while his crop wasted. He made things to please others, and smiled when they smiled, but never understood the use of what he made.

Now, since Asis was busy caring for his creation, Sebeni spent much of her time with Dirobo.

'Make something of your own, Dirobo,' she said to him

one day. 'Something you've never seen us make.'

Then Dirobo pulled grass stems through his hands and looked unhappy.

'Can't you do this?' asked Sebeni, and Dirobo chewed his lip, and his eyes filled with tears.

Then Sebeni mocked him. 'Perhaps you aren't as clever as you seem,' she said, and when his face twisted with pain she laughed long and loudly. And Dirobo ran away and hid among the trees.

When Asis returned he asked, 'Where's Dirobo?' and Sebeni told him.

'He's run away to be alone and sulk. He'll come back. He's nothing more than our reflection in the pool of life. He can't live alone.'

Dirobo had taken his unhappiness to the forest, and there he sat and grieved. But presently his quick eyes became busy, and he stood and tore a bough off a tree as he had seen Asis do when building poles were needed. He bent and released the bough, and felt the strength of the wood leap in his hand. He did this again and again, and pondered over it for a long time. Then he stripped the bark from the bough and plaited it as he had seen Sebeni plait grass. When, between his hands, he tried the rope he had made, he found it was very strong. Then his mind made a leap, and he strung the first bow. He plucked the taut bow-string, and it sang for him.

Then he found a place where lightning had fired the bush, and he touched some smouldering wood with his hand and it bit him. He backed away, sucking burnt fingers, and thought. Then he took a straight stick and touched the hot wood with this, and the fire crawled up the stick towards him. Hastily he beat it out, and ground the blackened end in sand to make sure the fire was gone.

When he touched this end with his finger he found it hard and sharp.

'This fire stuff is valuable,' he said. 'How can I keep it with me always?'

After he had considered he made a pot as he had seen Sebeni do. In this he placed some smouldering wood and carried it with him. When it seemed about to die, he blew, and it lived again.

And then, suddenly, there came to Dirobo a grand new thought that was wholly and entirely his own. He took his bow, the sharp stick, and the pot of fire, and stood up so that his eyes could search the horizon.

Now, some time later, the animals came angrily to Asis and said, 'This Dirobo is evil. He has a bow thing, and a sharp stick, and with these he kills us. And he takes our flesh, and burns it with fire that he carries in a pot. Afterwards he sits and eats what he has burnt. Is this what you intended, Asis?'

'By Creation, no!' shouted Asis, and beat his fist angrily against a thigh. 'I'll speak to this Dirobo.'

And he went off to do so.

But Sebeni smiled and said, 'So that Dirobo *was* clever. That is, after I had stirred him up.'

Asis strode about the earth in a temper shouting for Dirobo, and Dirobo heard him (he could scarcely avoid doing so), and hid. When Asis searched the forest he crouched in the grass of the veldt until the antelopes cried, 'Here he is, Asis!' Then Asis scoured the veldt, but Dirobo hid among the reeds. And when the buffalo told Asis to look in the reeds Dirobo took a hollow reed in his mouth, slipped into the lake, and lay under the water breathing through the reed. The fish, who could see him plainly, could not go on land to tell Asis where he was, for that was against their nature. Eh! But he was clever, that Dirobo.

Asis grew weary of the search, but the animals would not let him rest for cries and complaints. 'Asis! Asis! That Dirobo! He kills more and more of us every day!'

Then Asis hated what he had made, and he called the Spider to him.

'Spider,' he said, 'tell me what you can do.'

'I can make a web,' said Spider.

'Can you make a web that will reach from earth to sky?' asked Asis.

'I can make a web that will reach anywhere,' said Spider.

'Then do this,' commanded Asis. 'Make me a strong web from earth to sky.'

The spider began her task. Heavens, how she worked! But in a little month it was done, and the web stretched up, out of sight, light, strong and perfect, and beaded with dew in the morning.

Then, after Asis had tested it with his foot and found it held, he took his wife by the hand, and said, 'It's no longer possible to live on earth for the trouble that Dirobo causes. We'll leave it, and go to live in the sky. Come!'

Sebini replied, 'Perhaps that will be best. Eh! But that Dirobo! So clever and amusing. I didn't think he had it in him. But of course you're right. And the sky will be a new place. I wonder if it will be more interesting than earth was?'

So together they climbed the web to the sky, and Spider followed them, eating the web as he went, so that Dirobo should not follow. And they stayed in the sky, taking no further interest in their old home, obeying the rule which says that once something is made, it must be left to live its own life.

When Dirobo had watched them go he stood up in the reeds where he was hiding, and yawned and stretched.

'And now the earth is mine,' he said. And he took his bow and arrow, and pot of fire, and came out to make it completely so.

The Leopard

Many years ago, in Asembo, beside the lake, there lived a
girl whose name was Adero. She was beautiful. So beautiful
that men managed to find business to do in Asembo as
often as three times a week, just to look at Adero. Suitors?
She had them by the score. Every young man for miles

around wanted to marry her. And not only them, but even important chiefs who owned more than a hundred cows. They used to go to Adero's parents, and suggest, gravely, that young men were all very well in their way, but what was really needed for a son-in-law was someone of substance. With about a hundred cows. Like themselves, for instance.

It did not do them any good. Young or old, rich or poor, Adero turned up her pretty nose at the lot. She was interested in combs and beads, in fine skins sewn all over with the most delicately tiny cowrie shells, in swimming in the lake on hot afternoons with her friends, and arranging each other's hair in interesting patterns while they dried on the sand afterwards. But in husbands? Not one bit.

She became the talk of that part of the land, and her mother, who was proud of her daughter's good looks, began to worry.

Adero had a younger sister, and no one could have called her beautiful. Her name was Adongo, a thin-faced little creature who limped. But she was extremely good at listening, and she noticed everything. She rested her big, still eyes upon you when you talked, and listened so quietly, and perfectly, that you just had to go on talking. And when, at last, you stopped, she would make some tiny remark, such as, 'Do you know, that when you talk, the end of your nose twitches?' Then you knew that you had said too much. Not a comfortable person Adongo, but you could not deny that she was clever.

Now, one day, a new suitor for Adero arrived in Asembo. Nobody had ever seen him before. His name was Chui; he was tall and slim and strong, and he walked like a great, graceful cat. He came in a boat from the islands across the gulf, with a number of young men who were almost as handsome as he was. As was proper, his friends went to

Adero's parents, and suggested that Chui would make a suitable husband for their daughter.

The mother and father made enquiries. They could see that Chui was good-looking, but was he rich? He was. He owned a whole island, and cattle beyond number. And the dowry he offered to honour the marriage was more than generous, it fairly took their breath away.

Adero's mother talked seriously to her daughter. 'Now look here, my girl,' she said, 'it's high time you got married, and you'll never get a better husband than this.'

She need not have worried. The moment that Adero saw Chui she became quite dumb with wonder. She knew at once that this was the only husband for her.

So the dowry was paid, the wedding arranged, and everyone delighted. Except Adongo. Her eyes followed the handsome Chui as he smiled cat-like at her mother, as he danced gracefully at the feasts before the marriage, and she said, 'Well, I'm glad he isn't going to marry me.'

'What's wrong with him?' they asked in amazement.

'His ears are pointed,' she replied.

'Pointed! They're nothing of the sort. No one could be better . . . Oh, for goodness' sake!'

But later on, when they took a careful, cautious look, they found that it was quite true. The tops of his ears did go up in little points. Most odd.

'Well, I think that pointed ears are very attractive,' said Adero. 'And anyway, he's marrying me, not you. Why do you always try and spoil everything?'

Now, in Asembo, it was the custom at marriages that the bridegroom and his friends should pretend to carry the bride away from her home by force. And so, when the feasting and dancing was at its height, Chui suddenly swung Adero off her feet, and ran with her in his arms across the shore to his boat. She screamed loudly, as a good bride should do, and all her menfolk shouted that someone was stealing their sister, and ran in pursuit. Then Chui's friends leaped in their way, and everyone rolled fighting and laughing on the sand, while the women pretended to wail. By the time that everything was sorted out, the boat was far away on the lake, lost in the night, and Adero had gone to her new home.

Then all the men clapped each other on the shoulder. The drums began again, everyone's toes began to tap, and away went the dance more furious than ever.

'A very fine wedding,' said the old men over their beer. 'A very fine wedding indeed.'

For the next day there was another custom. A party of young girls, friends of Adero, set off to stay with her for a few days, so that she should not feel lonely among strangers. In the early morning, and dressed in their best clothes, they went down to the shore to cross to the island in the gulf. And there they found, waiting in the boat, little sister Adongo.

'What are you doing here?' they asked.

'I'm going too,' she said calmly.

Now this was most awkward because, as has been said, Adongo limped, and everyone knows that this kind of thing can bring very bad luck to a marriage. Adongo must have been aware of it, but she did not seem to think it mattered, and the other girls were far too good-natured to point out the difficulty to her. They tried a little persuasion.

'You don't want to go all that way in a dirty old boat,' they said.

'I do,' said Adongo.

'But we'll be gone for days,' they protested.

'I doubt it,' she replied, 'but, anyway, I'm going.'

So that was that, and without saying anything more the girls boarded the boat and paddled away to the islands.

When they arrived they were made much of: presents were pressed on them, a feast prepared, and they were shown a fine new hut to sleep in especially built for the occasion.

Adongo sniffed when she saw it.

'I'm not sleeping in that,' she declared.

'Well then, where are you going to sleep?' asked Adero, who was feeling bad-tempered because her sister had come at all.

Adongo looked round. 'I'll sleep there,' she said, pointing to a nearby hut.

'But that's where Chui and I sleep,' said Adero.

'It looks big enough for three,' replied her sister.

And in spite of anything anyone could say Adongo got her own way. That night, when Adero and her husband went to bed, Adongo was lying comfortably upon a sleeping mat at the far side of their hut.

'You see, there's plenty of room,' she said. 'Anyway, don't mind me. I'll be going home soon. Good night.'

Chui, growling angrily, went to his bed, and Adero to hers. Soon the hut grew quiet. The fire on the hearth burned low, sometimes flaring for a moment with tiny hesitant blue flames, then sinking again with a puff of falling ash. Adero was asleep. Across the hut from her Chui lay still. And Adongo watched.

Much later, outside in the night, an owl hooted twice, and she saw Chui stir. He raised his shoulders from the bed and stared across the hut. It seemed to Adongo that his shape grew first blurred, then heavy. Surely the neat pointed ears were longer now, even tufted. They twitched once, then again, and what had been a man was now a sleek, spotted leopard. The great head swung lazily in her

B

direction, and she saw the yellow eyes blaze in the firelight. Then they turned towards Adero, and the beast gathered himself to spring.

So Adongo coughed loudly. 'Hem!'

Have you ever seen a hungry leopard change his mind in mid leap, and try and turn himself into a man?

Neither have I. But it must have been a remarkable sight. Even amusing. He was so fussed that he got quite a lot wrong, stayed clumpy about the feet, and forgot about the whiskers that stuck out from his chops like steel wire. There may even have remained the suspicion of a tail. Fortunately the firelight was dim again now, and so he had time enough to get things straight and pass muster.

'What's the matter with you?' he snarled.

'Nothing. Nothing at all,' said Adongo sweetly.

'Well, go to sleep then,' he said, and half closed his eyes, and waited.

An hour later (and by this time he was really hungry) it seemed that everyone must be asleep. His bride was. In fact she was snoring; that is, if such a word can be used about a girl as beautiful as Adero. Snoring in a charming kind of way.

Cautiously, Chui began translating himself into his real shape. He raised a flat, tawny head from the bed-skin, licked his lips with a great wet tongue, and thrust out a careful paw. The talons slid like curved knives from their velvet sheathes. Then iron muscles bunched beneath the silken fur, and . . .

And that confounded girl across the room coughed again, 'HEM!'

'BLOOD AND MARROW BONES!' roared Chui. 'What's the matter now? Are we never going to sleep?'

'I'm extremely sorry,' she said, 'but I'm so thirsty that

it's impossible to sleep. There was far too much salt in that chicken stew.'

'Well, drink then!' he bellowed.

'But there isn't any water.'

'I'll get some,' he muttered, and got out of bed.

'I'm afraid it's not as easy as that,' she said. 'You see, I'm accustomed to only one kind of cup. Foolish of me, no doubt, and awkward for you. But there, everyone has their little peculiarities. This is mine.'

'What kind of cup?' he asked.

'A bird's nest.'

'A bird's nest!'

'Yes.' And then she added in a reasonable voice: 'It doesn't matter what kind of bird.'

'I'll get one,' he said. 'Anything for a little sleep.'

He padded cat-like out of the door and went looking for a bird's nest. As luck would have it he did not have to look far. Just outside the boma hedge there was a drift of old weaver-birds' nests hanging like fruit from the frail branches of a young camphor tree. He reached up and scooped one from its fork. It was shaped like a drinking gourd, with a curved neck. The very thing. At the lake edge he filled it brim-full of water, and started back to the hut.

Before he had gone two steps it was empty. He stared in amazement, then shrugged, turned back, and filled it again.

An hour later he was still filling that nest and trying to get the water home. He had changed into his leopard shape, since, this being his natural one, he found it easier to keep his mind upon the problem of keeping water in the nest. He carried it with his teeth so that he could run faster. No good. And he was wet through, which leopards hate just as much as cats.

I cannot help thinking that he was not a very bright leopard.

Finally he lost his temper.

'LIVER AND LIGHTS!' he bawled, and smashed the wet nest to the ground. 'Asleep or awake, I'll eat both of them!'

And he bounded soundlessly along the path to the hut to do so.

They were gone, of course. Little sister Adongo had seen to that. She had woken Adero the moment the leopard husband was out of the house, explained everything, and they had gathered their things hurriedly, and fled to where the girls slept in the fine new house. A moment later they all crept like shadows down the shore, pushed out the boat that lay stranded there, and paddled away. They were going home, through the night, to Mother.

'. . . and I've never been so deceived by anyone in all my life,' said Adero through her tears.

'There, there,' said Mother, clasping the girl to her bosom. 'A leopard, indeed! Whatever next? You know, I never did feel too sure about that young man. However, we *do* have the dowry. I don't see anyone coming to ask for *that* back.'

'That isn't how I heard it,' said little sister Adongo tartly.

What do you do about girls like Adongo?

Libina the Coward

Many years ago there lived five Masai brothers. Their names were Ole Scriani, Ole Tiptip, Ole Loitokitok, Ole Doinyo, and, the youngest, Libina. The four eldest of these were fine upright warriors, and sound about all those things which a good Masai should be. They were tall, sinewy, and strong, and, when they considered the matter, genuinely sorry for anyone who had the misfortune not to be born a Masai. They carried big spears, and could run for ever without feeling tired. They hunted lions, stole cows, loved fighting, smacked their lips over a good pot of milk and blood, and their proud, hawk-like faces seemed as if they might be carved from red stone.

Libina was not like this at all. He was rather fat, his legs were short, and his spear-work disgraceful. Also he very much disliked getting hurt. What he was good at was telling stories. 'Many years ago . . .' he would begin, and his face would grow serious and inward-looking, and, provided they had no fighting, hunting, or cattle-stealing on hand at the moment, his brothers would listen, and find it quite entertaining. Libina's stories, they said, were excellent for passing an idle hour pleasantly, but, of course, they had nothing to do with the real business of life. Also sometimes Libina seemed to mix himself up in his stories, and describe how he had done this brave, or dangerous, or exciting thing. This worried them.

'But, Libina, is this true?' they asked.

'Of course not,' he retorted furiously. 'It's a story.'

'Well, it sounds a lot like simple lying,' they said sternly. 'You should be careful, Libina. Some people might not understand.'

Now, Libina fell in love with a girl called Lika. She was pretty, and her father owned one of the biggest herds of cattle in the land. He was a stern old Masai of the most old-fashioned sort. You would not have thought that a girl like Lika, coming as she did from this kind of family, would have been interested in Libina, but she was. Perhaps she found her father, and all her sound Masai brothers, somewhat boring. Or perhaps it was Libina's stories, which could be most fascinating. Whatever the reason, she liked Libina, and was happy with him. But also, when she was alone, and thought about him, her face became sad. Because there could never be any question of her father allowing her to marry Libina. No question at all.

Libina's brothers soon noticed his interest in Lika, and, in the annoying way that elder brothers have, they talked to him sensibly.

'Look here,' said Ole Seriani, the eldest. 'It's no use you getting ideas about marrying Lika.'

'Why not?' asked Libina indignantly.

'Because it's quite impossible. Just couldn't happen. For one thing, you're not at all the kind of person her father would ever want as a son-in-law. For another, you haven't got the cows to pay the dowry. I'd say he'd want at least fifty for a girl like Lika, and you haven't got one.'

'Then I'd better begin getting them,' said Libina, 'because I *am* going to marry Lika. You're the experts on this, how do I do it?'

'Oh, come!' said Ole Tiptip. 'There's only one right and proper way to get cows. Steal them.'

'Right,' replied Libina, 'then I'll steal them. Now you must help me. Tell me how I steal cows.'

Tiptip laughed, but Ole Loitokitok said seriously, 'No, Brother. You shouldn't laugh. I know it's late, but the boy is at last showing interest in something that matters. We mustn't discourage him. There's a big raid against the Nandi planned for next month. Let him come with us, and perhaps he'll get a cow or two. Anyway, it will be good training, and much better for him than all this sitting around telling stories.'

So they found him a good spear, and Ole Doinyo, who was skilled at such things, spent a long time teaching him to make a hide shield that suited his grip. All the brothers took it in turns to speak about the tricks that made for success in cattle-raiding, and giving him practice with the spear.

Next month Libina went with them, and a large number of other young warriors, on the raid against the Nandi. They crossed the Nzoia River, up to their necks in swirling yellow water (they had to help Libina because it would have been over his head), and they marched for a day through the Nandi Forest. That night they slept in bracken beneath the trees. It rained hard, and there were elephants moving close by. Since they could not light fires without warning the Nandi, they had to stay awake to avoid being trampled to death. What with this, the rain, and his aching feet, Libina began to be sorry he had come, but he comforted himself with thoughts of cows and Lika, and did not complain.

Early next morning they sighted a large herd of Nandi cattle. After they had chased off the five or six herdsmen who guarded them they rounded up all the beasts, and began driving them home. But they had not been doing this for long, when, in front, a small army of Nandi stood up in the tall grass where they had been hiding, and blocked their path.

There was a great bustle among the Masai. Two men were left to watch the cattle, and the rest formed a line, Libina among them, with spears and shields ready.

'Now,' said Ole Tiptip, who was next to Libina, 'you're going to take part in a really good fight. Your first raid too. Aren't you lucky. Just the thing to put a polish on your training. Remember, keep your shield up, your spear down, and watch their eyes.'

There was no time for more instruction because at that

moment the Nandi gave an appalling scream and charged. And Libina took one look at them and ran. If he had not lost his way twice he would have done the journey home in about half a day. As it was he was still sitting outside his hut, puffing and exhausted, when his brothers arrived. They were furious.

'I wouldn't have dreamed that anyone in our family could behave in such a disgraceful . . .' began Ole Seriani, and then stopped because he felt that what he was saying was quite inadequate.

'Where's your shield?' snapped Ole Tiptip.

'I threw it away,' panted Libina. 'It was a nuisance while I was running.'

'HE THREW AWAY HIS SHIELD!' they shouted in chorus.

'Oh, what does it matter?' said Libina. 'It was only a bit of old bent wood and hide. I can easily make another.'

'The value of the thing has got nothing to do with it,' said Ole Loitokitok. 'It's the disgrace. A Masai either comes back from battle with his shield or on it. Throwing it away just isn't done. Really! Talk about explaining the obvious to a half-wit!'

'All right,' said Libina. 'So I ran away. But I'd no idea it was going to be like that. Why didn't you tell me? This fighting business is quite different in my stories. All that screaming, and those beastly black spears. I might have been badly hurt and . . .'

'The best thing you can do,' said Ole Seriani, 'in fact the only decent thing you can do, is to go away and never show your face near here again.'

'Well, if that's what you think, I will,' said Libina. 'But I'm going to see Lika first.'

He found her beside her father's cattle pen, weeping. Evidently the news had arrived before him. She could not

manage to say anything at all, only gazed at him with eyes
full of tears, and when, a little annoyed by her silence,
he told her that his brothers thought he ought to go away,
she just nodded, and burst into tears. So he left her.

He wrapped some food and a cooking pot in a bed-skin
and picked up an old simi.

'I suppose it will do for chopping wood,' he said bitterly,
as he strapped the sheath to his waist. 'I don't seem to be
very good at putting these things to their proper use.'

Then he slunk away without saying goodbye. He walked
all day across Naivasha Plain beneath the mountain, and
in the evening fell in with a party of Bukusu warriors
camped round a fire on the banks of the Nzoia River.

'Come and have some beer,' they shouted cheerfully.

So he sat down beside their fire and drank the beer.

'What's your name, Masai?' they asked.

And after he had told them they asked, 'Where's your
shield and spear?'

'Now, that's a long story,' said Libina.

'Stay, and tell it to us after we've eaten,' they said.
Then they pulled a joint of roast antelope off the spit and
shared it out. What with the beer and the good meat
Libina began to feel more himself again.

'Now, what about that story?' asked his hosts.

Libina's face became serious. His eyes fixed on the fire,
and he began the story. It was a long and exciting one,
full of fierce Nandi, and a battle that raged back and forth
all day, and cunning campaign tricks, and cattle pens
brimming with stolen cows of the highest quality. Far too
long for us to go into here, and you must take my word that
it more than adequately accounted for the missing shield
and spear.

When he finished the Bukusu first looked at him with

respect, and then questioningly at each other.

'Yes,' said their leader. 'Libina, you're just the man we want. Let me explain. We're camped here because we're waiting for the full moon, which happens tomorrow night. Then we are going to try and kill Eyabebe.'

'Eyabebe?' asked Libina. 'Who's he?'

'By Gogo, he doesn't know about Eyabebe!' they cried. 'Where have you been all your life?'

'Tell me,' said Libina.

And so they did. Eyabebe was a great snake. He lived under the mountain in a cave that was so deep a man could not possibly find an end to it. Once a month, on the night of the full moon. Eyabebe came from his cave, and ravaged the country for miles around. He ate anything living, cattle, men, anything. They went down Eyabebe's maw, and that was the end of them. When his hunger was satisfied the snake returned to his cave, and there, in the depths, he slept until the next full moon.

He caused great sorrow to the Bukusu people, for the land near the cave was crossed by fine streams from the mountain, and the grass was good. Just what was needed for their cattle. A man who built his house there would live well, but who could exist with Eyabebe breathing down his neck once a month?

'Now,' said the Bukusu leader, 'we're going to attempt to kill him. Many have tried before, and all failed, but perhaps we might succeed. And you're just the kind of man whose help we could do with.'

'Oh, no,' said Libina hastily. 'I'd like to, of course, nothing would please me better, but . . . well, as it happens, I've something important that I must do tomorrow . . .'

The Bukusu looked at him stonily.

'You were glad enough to eat our meat,' said one.

'You're a Masai, aren't you?' asked another.

'Oh, all right,' said Libina. 'I'll come.'

The Bukusu smiled. 'Of course you will,' they said. 'We realise that you were only joking.'

The next evening they moved across the plain to Eyabebe's cave. Libina's spirits rose and fell like a bucket in a well. At one moment he thought, 'It can't be as bad as fighting Nandi. Eyabebe's only a snake, and there's but one of him,' and he grew cheerful. And then he said, 'But he must be terribly big to eat all those cows and men,' and his smile became sickly.

As the moon was rising they reached a great cliff at the base of the mountain. By day its colour would have been a burning red, but in this light it was silver, and, to Libina's anxious gaze, it seemed to move as if the rock breathed. At its foot were deep mysterious shadows. The Bukusu showed him the cave mouth, a long narrow slit running up the cliff, hung with fern and creeper. They told him that only in the middle of this entrance was there room enough for the snake to pass. The men spread out near the cave, gripped their spears and simis, and waited.

And presently, far inside the mountain, they heard Eyabebe stir. There followed the slither and whisper of his progress through hidden passages, then suddenly a great head filled the hole, and cold eyes glinted in the moonlight. He roared savagely, once, and the bulky coils of his gigantic length writhed out as if they would never end.

'Oh, Mama, no . . .' moaned Libina in horror.

The snake swept the struggling Bukusu aside like grass stems, and then Libina ran.

He put a good five miles between himself and the cave, before sitting down to catch his breath.

'Well, that's that,' he said. 'I'm a failure, and not fit

to live with anyone. How I happened to be born a Masai I can't imagine.'

Then, worn out, he went to sleep in the grass.

In the morning he saw that he was in a small valley, with a stream running along its bottom. A pleasant place, hidden and quiet, with trees and reeds along the water's edge.

'I'll live here,' said Libina. 'Where there's nobody before whom I can disgrace myself. It would be nice, though, if there was someone to listen to my stories.'

He built a rough shelter and thatched it with reeds. He snared a hare or two, dug lily bulbs near the stream, robbed a wild bees' nest of its honey, and found a fig tree in fruit. There was food enough, and a home of sorts.

II

Several days later he was cooking a supper of hare and wild plantains when a shadow fell across the pot before him. Turning, he saw an old woman standing near. She was ragged and bent, her grey hair straggled in rat's-tails down her face; but her eyes, though sunken, were bright. Seeing her there so unexpectedly gave him a little shiver of surprise, but then he saw that she was just an old woman who looked tired and worn, as if she had travelled far, and eaten little.

'Hello, Granny,' he said. 'You startled me.'

She said nothing, but looked at the bubbling stew, licked her skinny lips, and held out a begging hand.

'So you're hungry, Granny. Well, so am I. It'll soon be ready and there's enough for two. Sit down. We'll have to dip out of the pot because I'm short of crocks.'

There was not much to the crone, skin and bones she looked to Libina, but she put away the best part of the stew, and scraped the pot with her fingers afterwards. Libina looked on with quiet dismay. He had reckoned on that food lasting two days, but he said nothing. The old creature must have been famished, and he was sorry for her. He would find something else tomorrow.

'Ah!' she said with satisfaction, and licked her thumbs. 'That's better.' Then she turned to him. 'You look a fine upright young man, and I know you're kind. What are you doing here, all by yourself in the wilderness, without even a wife to cook for you?'

'Well, the fact is, Granny,' he replied, 'I may look what you say I am, but it's not true. I'm what's known as a failure.'

'Tell me,' she said, and hitched closer.

Libina did. He told her about Lika and his brothers, and the raid on the Nandi. And about his disgraceful behaviour at Eyabebe's cave. Everything. When he had finished he felt better.

'So you see, Granny,' he said, 'it's as I said. I'm a failure and quite hopeless.'

'Hm,' she said, and looked him over speculatively. 'Tell me about Eyabebe.'

'There's nothing more to tell, Granny. He's just a terribly big snake, as thick as the chest of an ox, and as long as the way home on a dark and rainy night. And he lives in a cave. That's all there is to him.'

'No,' she said. 'I want to know more. How big is the cave, both in width and height? And how much room is there left when the snake comes out; above, below, and to either side? I must know everything, and be sure you get it right.'

So Libina first thought hard, and then carefully described Eyabebe's cave mouth.

'Hm,' said the old woman when he had finished, and for a

while she considered. 'Now,' she went on, and leaned her face close to his, 'listen carefully, because this is what you must do.'

Libina listened, and after a while drew back and muttered, 'Oh, no.'

A little later he cried loudly, 'No, no! I can't.'

And when at last she finished speaking he drew a deep breath, and said, 'Look, Granny, you've come to the wrong person. I thought I'd made it plain that I'm not a hero. You go and find someone better suited for a plan like that.'

The old woman gathered her rags and sat up straight. Her eyes glittered in a way that troubled him, and she asked sternly, 'Libina, are you a man or a rabbit?'

'A rabbit, Granny. That is, if being a man means doing what you want me to.'

'Bah!' she said. 'Look at me.'

He did so. She had strange eyes. A deep black, they were; black as a crow's breast feathers, and with little hard lights dancing in their depths. They held him, and he struggled. Presently he gave in, and muttered, 'All right, Granny. I'll try.'

For the next five days he worked hard. He found two sturdy cork trees, and felled them with his simi. Then he lopped the branches, and afterwards hewed the soft, spongy wood of their trunks into roughly the shapes of the upper and lower halves of Eyabebe's cave mouth. This done, he made two journeys to the cave, each time carrying one of the tree-trunks. His shoulders rubbed raw, the sweat smarted in his eyes, and the old crone hobbled beside him, and nagged. Sometimes he hated her beyond bearing. Was prepared to fling the timber down and give up. But when this happened she would suddenly smile sweetly, and he would curse, and grin in spite of himself, and go on.

By day the cave in the red cliff was quite another place. The grass at its foot was young and fresh, orchids hung from cracks in the rocks, and birds sang in nearby trees. Libina eyed the cave depths a little anxiously, but he knew it was safe. Eyabebe was asleep in the heart of the mountain, and would only come out at the full moon. There were two more days before that. He gave a further trimming to his tree-trunks, and afterwards, instructed by the old woman, he thrust them into the cave mouth, one up, and the other down. The narrowing rock walls bit into the cork, and they jammed hard, blocking the entrance except for a hole in the middle. They hoped this was large enough for the snake's head to pass through, but not the thickness of his body.

That done, they went home, and while Libina slept, the old woman carried his simi to the stream, and honed it sharp upon a rock. Maybe she said a spell or two over it, who knows?

On the night of the full moon they waited one each side of the cave entrance. Sometimes they spoke in whispers, but mostly they were silent. Libina twisted and gripped the simi in moist hands, and swallowed and swallowed at a lump which would not go down his throat.

And then, in the depths, the cave sighed. There was the rustle and scrape of Eyabebe approaching. The noise grew louder, the snake roared its blood-lust, and the echoes ran back and forth in the rock while the ground shook.

'I'm sorry, Granny,' cried Libina suddenly, 'I'm off! This is too much for me.'

'Stay!' she commanded. 'Think of Lika!'

'I do, Granny, but will Eyabebe?'

'Too late!' she cried. 'Look!'

He turned, and, horrified, he saw the snake's enormous flat head thrust out, all wicked curved fangs and evil eyes. Then the vast body smashed against the cork trees. He heard the tortured wood protest, saw it shudder, then hold. Gripped between the tree-trunks, Eyabebe bellowed with rage.

'Strike!' shrieked the crone, and with a sob Libina whirled back the simi, shut his eyes, and cut.

'Wheeh!'

And the head of Eyabebe fell bounding in the grass.

Then Libina walked ten paces from the cave mouth, sat down with his back to it, and felt very ill indeed.

When he was somewhat recovered, he got the severed head on his back with the help of the old woman. Then, stumbling beneath the weight, he started the journey to his proper home. The old woman followed.

On the way they met some of the Bukusu warriors who had tried to kill Eyabebe. Their jaws dropped when they saw his load, and they gasped, 'No!'

'Oh, yes,' muttered Libina, and trudged on.

At home he flung down what he carried before his astonished brothers. They gaped.

'That's Eyabebe's head!' they exclaimed.

'Right,' said Libina. 'I killed him. And now, please will somebody take the awful thing away. I'm sick of it.'

'Who helped you?' asked Ole Tiptip suspiciously.

'Nobody,' said Libina, 'Oh, well, yes. There was somebody. An old woman.'

His brothers fell about with laughter. 'An old woman! An old woman helped you kill Eyabebe! Eh, Libina. This is a new and better light we see you in, but you haven't lost your old sense of humour.'

'But there *was* an old woman. She gave me a lot of good ideas. She's here, behind me . . . Well, she *was* here. Where is she?'

He never saw her again. Somewhere, between the cave and home, while Libina was bent beneath the weight of Eyabebe's head, she vanished. For ever.

And Libina could never make anyone believe that she had existed. It used to make him very cross.

'You know,' he said to his wife years later, and for the hundredth time, 'there *was* an old woman.'

'Yes, dear,' replied Lika.

King Lion

You know, some people have a number of quite wrong ideas about the lion. He is supposed to be kingly, and noble. Well, he is not. Big, certainly, and good-looking in a heavy way, but also very lazy, and a terrible bully. He lies around for days on end, yawning and sleeping. The yawn is the kind that threatens to split a head in two. It also reveals a mouthful of unpleasantly yellow teeth. His wife does the hunting while he looks after the children. Or, rather, sleeps in the middle of them, and hits out hard when they wake him up. If she brings home something to eat, then he does wake up. Enough to make certain of the first helping, and heaven help anyone else in the family if they try to take a mouthful while he is eating. Once full, the others may have what is left, usually hide and bones. King Lion is asleep again.

Now if this is a king, then he is not a very good one, and if that is nobility, I prefer something else.

The people who live round the Great Lake have many stories about lions, and all of them show that they have a shrewd idea what kind of a person Lion is. Listen to one of them, and see what you think.

Lion was king, and he had many servants. He lived on the flat top of a large ant-heap somewhere in the plain near M'balageti, for the grass grew thick and soft there, and made a fine bed. When he was awake he could lift his great head, and stare across miles of flat-topped thorn and ochre sedge. A fine prospect, and he was right in the middle of it. Then he would roar for food (on a moonlit night, when the wind was right, you could hear him at far Ngorongoro), and his servants came running.

Now, one day they were all late, and when they did arrive, all fussed and puffed, Lion was in an atrocious temper.

'Are you all here?' he asked, and looked them over with a cold eye.

'Yes, King Lion,' they squeaked. 'All present. Every one.'

'Good,' he said. 'Now listen. In order to improve the service I'm going to make a small change in the way things are done. It's been inconsiderate of me to make all of you come with the food. You're overworked.'

'What condescension,' they murmured anxiously. (They knew their master.)

'Yes,' he continued, 'we'll stop that from now on. In future only one animal will bring it. A different animal each day. And he won't have anything to carry BECAUSE HE'LL BE THE FOOD! I'll eat him. Is that understood?'

'Yes, King Lion,' they wailed unhappily.

'Right,' he said. 'The next meal is at midday tomorrow. Go away, and decide among yourselves who's going to bring it. It should be a very interesting discussion. Now, GET OUT!'

So they all tumbled helter-skelter down the ant-heap and away across the plain to the meeting place beside the River M'balageti.

King Lion was right. It was an interesting discussion. There were present, Hare, Impala, Ant Eater, Wart Hog, Duiker Buck, Dik-dik, Dassie, Cane Rat, Mongoose, Wildebeest, Bush-baby and Baboon, all of them usually talented and interesting speakers. For an hour they sat and looked at each other from the corners of their eyes and said nothing. Silence? You could have cut it up like cake.

Finally Baboon gave a great sigh, and said, 'Well, this isn't going to get us far. How do we decide who goes first?'

Wildebeest said, 'We could draw lots. Let me explain. You do it with straws. Somebody bites off a lot of straws of the same length. Except for one straw, which he makes shorter. Then he holds all of them so that no one can see which is the short one, and we all choose . . .'

'Who holds the straws?' asked Dik-dik.

After a pause, Wildebeest said, 'Yes.'

There was another very long silence.

'I know,' said Wart Hog. 'We could do it by means of a slow race. The opposite to an ordinary race. We all start together, and the one who gets to Lion *last* wins.'

'And the one who gets there first?' asked Cane Rat.

And Wart Hog in his turn said, 'Yes.'

'Besides,' said Duiker Buck morosely, 'that way, nobody would ever get there at all. Can you imagine King Lion when that happened?'

They could, and did, and shuddered.

Then, along the river bank came Ground Squirrel. He is a delightful little animal. Slim and sleek, with a neat grey coat, he flits across ground like some engaging clockwork toy, then stops and stands and peers and laughs. He did it now.

'What's the matter with all of you?' he asked.

'Where were you this morning when King Lion roared for food?' they demanded.

'Busy,' said Ground Squirrel. 'There are always too many of us anyway. I took the day off.'

'Well, you missed something,' said Bush-baby. And they explained.

'. . . and we haven't decided anything yet,' said Ant Eater. 'Quite frankly, I don't see us ever doing so.'

'I'll go,' said Ground Squirrel.

'WHAT?' they shouted.

'Have you any objections?' he asked.

'Oh, no,' they said hurriedly. 'None at all.'

And so the next day Ground Squirrel presented himself as a meal for King Lion. He arrived about two hours late and he could hear the king roaring with rage long before he reached him. When, at last, Squirrel flickered up the side of the ant-hill King Lion bellowed, 'you . . .!' And then he went on thundering while Squirrel waited patiently to get a word in edgeways.

When this was possible he said, 'I know I'm late and no one could be more sorry. But I was delayed.'

'Delayed!' shouted Lion. 'How?'

'On my way here,' explained Squirrel, 'I met a Creature. He stopped me, and said that I shouldn't come at all. I told him that I knew my duty even if he didn't. He replied that *he* wouldn't go to get eaten by any stupid lion, king or not. Well, I said at once, that I'd never heard a more irresponsible remark and that . . .'

'Creature?' asked King Lion savagely. 'What creature?'

'Now that I can't say,' said Squirrel, 'because he was a complete stranger to me. However, I said . . .'

'Where is he?' demanded Lion.

'The Creature? By the river,' said Squirrel. 'But forget him. I'm sure you're hungry.'

King Lion heaved himself to his feet. 'Take me to that Creature,' he said ominously.

Squirrel stared. 'What, all the way to the river?' he asked. 'Yes.'

'But you never leave your royal ant-heap.'

'Will you do as you're told?'

'Oh, all right,' said Squirrel. 'I can't promise that he'll still be there. However, if that's what you want, follow me.'

He led the way across the plain, and behind him stalked King Lion muttering to himself, 'Confounded insolence . . . teach him a lesson. . . . Creature indeed . . .' and, from their hiding places in the wait-a-bit thorns, Hare, Impala, Ant Eater, Wart Hog, Duiker Buck, Dik-dik, Dassie, Cane Rat, Mongoose, Wildebeest. Bush-baby and Baboon watched him pass, and sucked in their breath with awe.

The M'balageti River winds in great loops, and for most of the year it is not so much a river as a string of still, reed-fringed pools. Squirrel led King Lion to a high bank over-looking the deepest of these and stared down.

'He's still there,' he said, and pointed.

Lion bounded beside him and looked into the water below. In it an enormous tawny creature wavered vaguely and looked up.

Lion snarled, and the Creature bared a row of awful yellow teeth in reply.

'AAARRR!' shrieked King Lion, beside himself with rage, 'I'll settle your hash!'

With that he plunged into the deep pool to do so. And drowned.

'And a very good riddance to a stupid, noisy, bore,' said Ground Squirrel, as he went home without once looking back.

Omolo and Sabala

Omolo was a Samia fisherman, and he came from Usenge,
a tiny village on the Kavirondo shore of the Great Lake.

You should see the place.

Inland, a vast waste of marshes with pale green papyrus
flowers nodding over them; along the shore, knolls of open

ground, and fine firm sand at the water's edge. There is an occasional fig growing, or a gnarled morabe tree with its strange, sausage-like fruit, heavy and hard, each dangling at the end of a long green stalk. The men of Usenge use them to flavour their beer. The huts straggle along the shore in a haphazard line, deep in a clutter of wide-bellied pots, foraging hens, rapacious goats, children, and gardens overflowing with pumpkin vines. The nets are spread to dry on the sand, and the water birds walk stiff-legged over them, searching for tails and scales and heads of fish. It is untidy and delightful, but when you see it there is always at the back of your mind a feeling that something uncanny could happen here.

Stranded on the sand are a rank of boats, and these are not untidy. Worn, sun-bleached, unpainted; yes. But carefully repaired, and their gear, baler, paddles, gourd for drinking water, sail-needle, and twist of sisal twine, all in the right places. The sails are exquisitely patched and carefully furled. On land the fishermen may be a feckless drunken lot, but with the boats they take no chances.

Across the water are a few islands and the far shore of the Gulf. Floating high in the sky are always two fish-eagles, huge white birds, proudly, effortlessly graceful. West, although you would never know it because the two shores interlock like coiled snakes, is a narrow strait that leads to the open lake. And through this, each night, the boats slip out to fish.

Omolo lived there a great time ago, but it will not have changed much.

There is a tale told of his birth. He was born sickly, and it seemed unlikely that this silent, scarcely breathing baby would live. His mother wept because all the children born to her in the past had died, and she was growing old.

That night she walked down to the shore, empty now, the boats gone to the fishing grounds; for, come what may, if life is to go on, fish must be caught. She faced the dark water and said, 'If you let my child live, I'll give him to you.'

For those who live by and beside it, the lake is more than just water, and a livelihood. She spoke to the spirits of the place.

Then, as nothing happened, she gave a sob, and returned to her sick child. Beside the bed-skin on which Omolo lay there squatted an old woman.

'Who are you, Granny?' Omolo's mother whispered, but she knew.

'You called us,' answered the old woman. 'We accept what was offered.'

Then she got stiffly to her feet and began to leave the hut. But at the door she paused, and said, 'The child will live.'

She went out into the night and vanished. And Omolo lived, and grew strong, laughing, brave, and skilled at anything to do with boats.

Far across the lake, in the distant Sese Islands, the senior wife of the king's governor wept in her house. Because she was childless she was despised by her husband, and mocked by his other wives. That night she walked from the governor's great household down to the shore, until the water coldly lapped her feet.

'If you give me a child I will make it yours,' she said to the darkness. She came from a lakeside clan, and the old beliefs cling hard.

When her first child, a girl, was born, she wrapped it in a costly cotton cloth, and took it to show her husband. Crossing the wide, bare compound to the governor's house, she was stopped by an old woman.

'A fine child,' said the crone.

The senior wife's throat grew dry. 'Who are you, Mother?' she whispered. But she knew.

'I don't need to tell *you* that,' said the old woman. 'We accept what you offered.'

The governor's wife hurried on to her audience, but she looked back once, and the old woman had vanished.

The girl grew graceful, laughing, and beautiful. They called her Sabala.

Later, much later, times were unusually hard upon the Kavirondo coast. The rains failed, or were thin, four years in succession. The people of Usenge had fish, and so they did not starve, but little else could be said for life in those years. Omolo, now a young man, and, since his mother was dead, having no other mouth than his own to fill, decided to look elsewhere for fortune. So he, and three other men of a like mind, took Omolo's boat, and sailed west to the Uganda shore. There they fished, sometimes having to fight for the right to throw a net on fishing grounds where they were strangers, and sold what they caught in the Buganda markets. They drank palm beer, were amazed at the size of the headache that followed, gambled for cowrie shells, danced, fell in and out of trouble as young men do, and moved on swiftly when it seemed too serious to be laughed off. In time they reached Sese, as poor as they began, owning nothing more than the boat, a spear apiece, and youth.

Now, the Lake Kingdoms were seldom peaceful, but this was a year of unusual upheaval. They seethed with war like a boiling pot, and the governor of Sese needed every spear he could command or buy. Omolo and his companions took service with him for their porridge, and they fought in the wars as far away as distant Ankole, where Omolo earned both reputation and respect as a warrior.

When the fighting was over he returned to Sese. Only one of his companions remained, a man called Aruwa, who was very close to Omolo. The other two were dead in Ankole. Omolo and Aruwa took places among the governor's household warriors, and it was now that Omolo first saw the governor's daughter.

It happened at a great feast. Omolo sat among the warriors; Sabala served her father's guests; and their eyes met. For the rest of that night Omolo did not taste his meat or hear any nearby talk, while Sabala poured beer in a trance. Across the Great Hut their eyes met, and looked away, and helplessly returned, and stayed. When the feast was nothing but picked bones on the floor, Omolo went to his hut sober, and Sabala fled to her bed and wept.

From that night they began to meet.

In a household such as this nothing remains unknown for long. If no one else sees and talks of it, then the ants in the walls and lizards in the thatch know and speak. Or so it seems.

A week later Aruwa suddenly spoke to Omolo across the boat they were scouring. He said, 'It would be wiser if you forgot this girl.'

'How did you know?' asked Omolo.

'Bah!' said Aruwa, and spat on the sand. 'I think the very fish in the lake know.'

'I'll die before I forget her,' said Omolo.

'You'll die if you don't,' said Aruwa. 'It's just a question of when. Go on as you are, and it will be very soon. Also, the way of it won't be pleasant.'

At about the same time the governor called Sabala to him and told her, 'It's time you were married. In two days

I'll send you as a wife for the governor of Mpiga. He's wanted you for a long time, and while I always thought well of the alliance, I never considered the dowry he offered to be large enough. Circumstances change. A cow or so, more or less, now seems of little importance to me.'

Sabala said, 'I will not become the wife of Mpigi. He's old, and already has many wives.'

When he had beaten her the governor said, 'It seems that your mother failed to teach you obedience. But then she was an unsatisfactory woman in many ways. And don't rest any hopes on that Samia fish-gutter, Omolo. His usefulness is over.'

Sabala cried, 'I'll marry only one man. Omolo. I'll take poison before I marry that goat you try to force on me.'

Somehow, that very night, Sabala slipped away unnoticed by the women set to watch her, and Omolo escaped the men searching for him. They hurried hand in hand through the night to the shore, and found there a man sitting on the sand with his back against the boat. Omolo raised his spear, and Aruwa said, 'Don't kill me, Omolo. I may be useful.'

'You've no need to meddle in this,' Omolo told him, and Aruwa replied:

'None at all. But I'm tired of this place and would like to see Usenge again. Also it occurred to me that someone must steer when you two have to paddle.'

But as they were talking there came shouts, and the pad of running feet, and Sabala's father with a pack of his household warriors were upon them. Shouting to Aruwa and Sabala to launch the boat, Omolo went up the beach like a lion. Two men lay groaning on the sand, the rest hanging back, and the governor raving behind them, when Aruwa cried that the boat floated, and Omolo ran to it. He had one leg over the side when a man up the beach shouted to the rest to give him room. Turning, Omolo saw that he was an archer, a man from the Katonga marshes who, alone in the Kingdoms, use the bow in war. The cord sang, the archer reached forward, watching the arrow fly, and Aruwa fell across a gunnel with a deadly little feathered finger pointing from his back. Then, with the strength of despair, Omolo flung his heavy war spear, and heard one cry before he thrust the boat into open water, and climbed aboard. On land a knot of men grouped silently round a still figure on the sand. Omolo had killed the king's governor.

Beyond the land's shelter there was wind. Omolo set the wide, three-cornered sail, and they ran before it. Sabala had taken the steer-board—the island women were no strangers to boats—and Aruwa lay huddled on the nets piled at her feet. The free corner of the sail once lashed down, Omolo went to him, and studied the wound silently. The arrow was clear through, the iron head had broken skin on his chest.

'It must come out,' he said in a troubled voice to Aruwa.

Grey-faced in the moonlight, his friend looked up. 'Why bother?' he asked. 'If it stays in I die, and if you take it out I die. There's no problem. I shall not see Usenge again.'

'I did this to you,' said Omolo with bitter grief.

'Yes,' said Aruwa. 'You and the woman, both. I suppose you could say that. But I saw your faces at the feast, and I'm not inclined to blame you. I think the lake had a hand in this. I'll ask her when she takes me.'

Aruwa died before dawn, and they gave him to the lake. Afterwards there was nothing to do. The wind was steady, the boat sailed herself. They waited silently to see what the day brought.

When there was enough light Omolo stood on a gunnel, steadied himself against the mast, and, beginning west, drew his gaze slowly across the horizon. He lingered for a moment on a huddle of distant sails, and then dismissed them. They were fishing boats making for the Kome Channel, and home, after the night's work. A moment later he said, 'Ah!', and pointed south. There were nine sails, spread wide, but within shouting distance of each other. Nine Sese war canoes.

'Of course,' said Sabala. 'We've killed my father, the king's governor. If necessary the clan will follow us to the ends of the earth. And they'll never give up.'

'That may be so,' said Omolo, 'but I see no reason why they shouldn't work for their revenge. It isn't easy to get the better of a Samia fisherman in a good boat.'

Wind was king. While it held the Sese boats could do little better than Omolo's light craft. But, if it dropped, each of them had ten paddles to his two. They went north-east, making for the creeks of the great papyrus marshes near Entebbe, and all day the lake gave them wind. Even so, when at dusk they nosed into the maze of waterways that spread between twelve-foot walls of dense reeds, the war canoes were close enough for the men in them to be counted. The marshes killed the wind, Omolo furled his sail, and laid the unstepped mast in the bottom of the boat. Then they paddled into a hot world of whispering grasses.

That night, deep in the marsh, they slept in each other's arms, but before dawn Omolo was cutting a path inland through the reeds.

'We leave the boat then?' said Sabala.

'No,' answered Amolo. 'We take it with us.'

'You're joking.'

'Never less. There'll be a creek somewhere, running level, back to open lake. Once afloat in that, with luck we lose them. They'll take half a day to find we're gone. They won't easily lug war canoes overland, and by the time they find we've gone it should be too late for them to get back to the lake before dark. Come now, let's work.'

For hours they cut reeds, and inched the boat through mud and over broken, oozing papyrus stems. The grass blades cut like knives, and in that stifling airless place the sweat mingled with blood, and they gasped for air. After a while they smelt fire, and presently heavy clouds of smoke blotted out the sky.

'They've fired the reeds,' said Sabala.

'Yes,' said Omolo. 'If it reaches us before we find water then indeed that's the end of it. But also it cuts our way. They can't get to us while the fire lies between.'

When at last they slid the boat through weed into green scum-covered water the wall of fire raged a few spears' lengths behind, and every breath seared their lungs. Omolo took the baling gourd and scooped water over both of them. Then they paddled swiftly down narrow creeks. At dusk the reeds opened, fell away to either side, and a cool wind kissed their grateful flesh. With sail hoisted they made east, as near into the wind as the boat allowed.

'We must find food,' said Omolo. It was two days now since they had eaten.

By morning they were far along the coast and no sign yet of pursuit. They sailed past a shore village, beached the boat, and Omolo went back carrying Sabala's heavy copper arm bangle to see what could be bought. The people were lake Busoga, heavy suspicious men, whose eyes lit up greedily at sight of the bangle. They gave him a stem of

C

bananas, a bag of casava flour, and a string of dried fish for it. Then, suddenly, after some muttered conversation among themselves, they offered to add sweet potatoes, which, they explained, he must give them time to dig. Omolo said he was content with what he had, and, when they showed signs of delaying him, brought up Aruwa's spear. So they let him go.

They sailed to a small island, grounded the boat, and dragged it inland to the cover of a tangle of stunted thorns. Then they cooked and ate a meal. Just before dark they watched nine Sese war boats sail past, making east.

They stayed three days on the island. 'Let *them* put distance between us,' said Omolo, and on the second night they went fishing and took a great catch. Sabala laughed to see the plump lake perch fall shining into the boat.

'By rights,' explained Omolo, 'a fisherman's wife should never see fish caught. It brings bad luck. But in your case we'll make an exception.'

'By rights,' said Sabala, 'the husband of the daughter of a king's governor should not be a fisherman. But in your case we'll make an exception.'

The three days gone, they went slowly along the coast, sleeping upon small islands, living on fish, and frugally eking out the flour. It was a week before they raised Rusinga to the south, ran through the straits into the Kavirondo Gulf, and turned north towards Usenge.

'Tonight my clan will feast a new daughter,' said Omolo, but when they were close enough to see he stared silently. The huts were blackened ruins, the reed fences of the gardens broken, crops trampled, and two boats lay gutted on the strand.

'First Aruwa, then this,' he said. 'Everyone pays my debts.'

His clan received him silently. That night Omolo ate dried fish and cold millet cake with Opio the clan elder, and the old man apologised for the meagerness of the food.

'Poor hospitality for a son come home,' he said, 'but we're hard hit. The huts are nothing; once rebuilt we'll be better housed than we were. But Atinga and Toll lost boats, and the crop is gone. We'll eat only fish again this year.'

Later he said, 'They came in the evening, and we saw them far out. Knew who they were before they were close enough to see the booms hung Sese fashion. You see, Omolo, your news had already reached us. We heard it on the fishing grounds and knew what to expect. We were lucky. Had time to get inland to the marsh, and the boats hidden at Rusinga.'

And lastly he stared shamefaced at his feet and said quietly, 'You must go away, Omolo. You and the woman. A king's governor dead, and his daughter stolen. They'll never give up. Forgive me, Omolo, but I must think for the clan.'

Omolo answered, 'There's nothing for me to forgive, Baba.'

The old man put out a thin hand. He had more to say. 'We don't blame you, Omolo. We've seen the girl, and we believe the lake had a hand in this. The women say so. There's talk among them of something only they know.'

'Yes,' said Omolo. 'Aruwa also believed it.'

Next day his clan stored the boat with food they could ill afford and watched silently while it sailed once more for the open lake.

'We'll try for the Mwanza shore, right across the lake,' Omolo told Sabala.

The day was overcast yet stifling, with heavy, dark-

bellied clouds piled to the north. The great rains had
been gone a month, but on the lake they often return.
There, weather is difficult to predict, and the seasons often
muddled. That night lightning flared continuously, and the
wind dropped, then blew in sharp squalls, then dropped
again. The day came late and sickly and with it the wind,
fresh and blusterous. The sail lines hummed like a great
harp. North, there were nine distant sails. No need to ask
whose.

'We carry too much sail for comfort,' said Omolo, 'but
with those dogs' noses down after us it must be risked.'

The boat ran swiftly, like a great bird. The lake was
up in heavy oily waves which sometimes broke over them,
and while Omolo hugged the kicking steer-board, Sabala
bailed. The Sese boats also kept their sails full, and gained
slowly. At noon the world grew dark, the wind dropped and
rain came down like a wall. Omolo knew what was coming,
and, while Sabala held the oar, and both drowned in icy
rain, he clawed down the sail and tried with a paddle to
turn the boat. He was too late. With Aruwa to help he might
have got her round in time, but now, when it came, the
wind seized them broadside on, in giant hands. It flung
them up, the mast shattered and was gone, the waves
roared in and over, and Omolo dragged himself along the
upturned boat searching for Sabala. Found, and imprisoned
between his arms, he locked both hands on a thwart, shut
his eyes and clung.

Much later, half drowned, the wind gone and the world
rinsed grey, he heard the wreck grate aground, and his
feet touched bottom. Carrying Sabala, he splashed ashore,
and they rested side by side on wet sand.

Presently he got to his knees and looked round. It was
the smallest fragment of land, sand and rock, and at its

greatest height a tangle of fleshy lake aloes. During a storm the spray would cover it. There are hundreds of such islands, always being found and lost again. Only lake crabs live on them, eating the feathers and droppings of visiting birds.

He walked to the water's edge and inspected the shattered boat. It lay on its side, emptied, mast and steer-board gone, the sewn seams gaping. Then he heard a distant shout, and out in the lake were the Sese boats paddling to shore. Only four of them now, he noted grimly, but it was enough.

He returned to Sabala, drew her up to stand beside him, and they waited. And as they watched the quick rise and dip of ranked paddles, an old woman came from the aloes.

'It's time,' she said gently, 'and long past the time for the lake to claim what was offered.'

The Sese warriors ran their keels through shallowing water until they checked in sand. Then iron clattered on drum-taut hide as they dropped paddles and reached for spears and shields. At the noise two great fish-eagles rose side by side from the island, and soared to endless freedom in the lake sky.

They never found Sabala and Omolo.

Zebra

Long ago, none of the animals that live by eating grass or leaves had horns, and because of this they were in great distress. They were so hunted by lions, leopards, hyenas and wild dogs that there was no time to eat. No sooner had a bushbuck or eland got his head down to a tasty patch of grass, or a giraffe or kudu his head up to a branch covered in young leaves, than somebody yelled, 'Lion! Run!' And they had to. Fast. They were missing more meals than they ate, and it made them wretchedly thin.

When this state of affairs had gone on far too long, somebody (it might have been Duikerbuck, who has sense) suggested that they must all meet to discuss what should be done. And this they did.

They gathered beneath a fine fig tree in the middle of a desert, where you could see anything move for miles, posted a couple of young antelope on high ant-hills to keep watch and began.

First, they wanted an animal to keep order and see everyone had a chance to speak, and the choice was easy. They gave wise Elephant the job. When Elephant says 'Shut up!', you shut up.

After that there was an interruption because Dik-dik, who is the smallest of buck, found himself sitting next to a jackal, and was not at all comfortable about it.

'Ought he to be here?' he piped loudly.

'I don't know,' answered Elephant. 'Who is supposed to be at this meeting, anyway?'

'It's a meeting of the Society of Grazers and Browsers,' said Hartebeest. 'Animals who eat just grass or leaves,' he explained for the benefit of the smaller buck.

'Good. Now we know,' said Elephant. 'Jackal, do you eat grass or leaves?'

'I eat anything,' replied Jackal.

'DISGUSTING !' they all shouted.

'Out!' said Elephant, and Jackal slunk off. 'You wait until I tell my friend Lion,' he snarled as he went.

Next they called a roll. Present were,

Buffalo
Bushbuck
Dik-dik
Duikerbuck
Eland
Elephant
Giraffe
Hartebeest
Impala
Kudu
Oribi
Reedbuck
Rhino
Roan
Sable
Wildebeest
                    and
                        Zebra.

Now, having settled all this in a sensible and business-like fashion, they got down to the main purpose of the meeting. What should be done about all those lions, leopards, hyenas and wild dogs?

'The whole problem is this,' said Wildebeest. 'We can't fight these creatures because we aren't built for it. So we have to run. And while we're running we can't eat. And since we can't eat we . . .'

'Oh, get on,' they shouted. 'We know all this.'

'Silence!' said Elephant, and when he had got it he asked Wildebeest, 'Have you finished?'

'What I want to say,' said Wildebeest stubbornly, 'is that we need some weapons. Like the animals which hunt us.'

'Now, that's sense,' said Kudu. 'A good mouthful of big, curved, sharp-pointed teeth, like Lion. That would keep them off.'

'Have you ever tried eating grass or leaves with a mouthful of curved, sharp-pointed teeth?' asked Oribi.

'No,' said Kudu.

'Neither have I,' said Oribi, 'but I should think it would be difficult.'

And after he had considered, Kudu said, 'Yes, I hadn't thought of that.'

'Well, let's have claws then,' suggested Dik-dik. 'About so long. With points as sharp as wait-a-bit thorns, and a good knife edge to them. That would make Leopard sit up.'

'And after half a day's grazing on the hard veldt it would make you sit down,' observed Buffalo. 'You'd have pretty sore feet with things like that sticking out of them.'

'Mm,' said Dik-dik. 'Hadn't occurred to me.'

Here Zebra stood up. So far he had been silent, and he never does say much. Rather a grumpy animal.

'A complete waste of time,' he said. 'I've never heard so much clotted nonsense in all my life. I should be eating, and that's what I'm going to do. Now.'

And he clattered off.

They watched him go in silence. It occurred to most of them that they also could be doing some solid eating. They were hungry.

'Look,' said Elephant with a sigh. 'We don't seem to be getting very far. I suggest that you let me go and see the god Khakaba. I'll tell him about your troubles and ask him to help.'

'Agreed!' they all shouted, and scuttled off back to the grass and leaves.

'Meeting closed,' said Elephant to nobody at all, and he lumbered off to see Khakaba.

Khakaba is not a god whom it is easy to deal with. Irritate him, and he is apt to give you toothache or make your hair drop out. Really annoy him, and you get army worm in your corn, and a flood thrown in for good measure. Even Elephant treats him respectfully. Fortunately, Khakaba seemed in a good humour, and listened quite patiently while Elephant explained about the trials of the grazers and browsers.

'I understand,' said Khakaba. 'What would satisfy them?'

'We-e-ll,' said Elephant. 'Teeth like Lion's are no good because of the food they eat. Leopard's claws would be a nuisance on hard ground. It did cross my mind that if they had some kind of large teeth, or claws, on their heads, where they wouldn't be in the way, that might answer.'

'You mean horns,' said Khakaba.

'Do I?' asked Elephant.

'Yes, you do,' said Khakaba, 'although I suppose that you were not to know, since I've just invented them.'

'When could we have these horns?' asked Elephant.

'Now, careful,' said Khakaba, 'I won't be hurried.'

'Yes, but it's rather urgent and . . .'

'Don't badger me,' bellowed Khakaba. 'You want lumpy-skin disease or something?'

'No,' said Elephant hastily. 'Then I'll leave it to you.'

But as he was leaving Khakaba growled, 'I'll put the whole lot under the fig tree in the middle of that desert by the night of the next full moon. They can fit themselves.'

'Thank you, Khakaba,' said Elephant, and went away to spread the good news.

So on the appointed night all the eaters of grass and leaves hurried across the desert to get their new horns.

Except Zebra. A family of reedbuck passed him on their way. He was as thin as a painted hat-rack, head down, but with one eye cocked for Lion, morosely eating as if his life depended on it. As, indeed, it did.

'Aren't you coming to the meeting place to get these new horn things?' they called.

'Hrrumph!' he said testily. 'Haven't time for nonsense of that kind.'

He snatched another mouthful of eragrostis, and they left him.

At the tree it was like dressing-up time at a good party. There was this enormous pile of horns, and when Elephant said 'Go!' they grabbed. Those who got an odd pair sorted it out afterwards by agreement. Horns of every description: curved like scimitars (Waterbuck), twisted like corkscrews (Kudu got a magnificent pair of these), massive and spreading (just right for Buffalo), tiny, straight and sharp as daggers (if Oribi lowers his head at you, run; his horns are like this). It is true that some of the buck ladies did not get any, but as Wildebeest said, 'It's up to the men to do the fighting anyway. Isn't it? What!'

Wildebeest is a gentleman of the old school.

Finally, only a pair of enormous tusks which no buck could lift were left on the ground. Elephant picked these up and stuck them in his cheeks, and their pale ivory gleamed in the moonlight.

As all hurried home in twos and threes, they passed Zebra, and he looked at them, first with astonishment, and then with growing resentment.

'I've been misled,' he said.

Then, 'It's unfair!'

And finally, 'I'm not going to put up with it!'

He went to see Khakaba, who was not pleased.

'At great inconvenience to myself,' said the god danger-ously, 'I put an enormous pile of heavy horns where I said I would. Do I also have to pick up a pair and stick them in you?'

'Unfair!' shouted Zebra. 'Look at me! Skin and bones! Never get time to eat for having to run away. I'm worn out. The others got a present of horns. Why not me? Unfair!'

'Great Creation!' roared Khakaba. 'I'll give you presents. You're thin, are you? I'll make you fat. And your mind runs on eating, does it? Here's a lip to fit your appetite, as well as your impudence. Now GET OUT!'

And Zebra went sadly back to his eating, a changed animal. He had been thin, now he was fat. And he scooped away at the grass with an enormous lower lip, a lip like a big, black, rubber satchel. It gathers in about a bushel at a time.

I think that this story might be true, because, almost alone among the browsers and grazers, he is without horns. And even in the worst of famines, when everyone else is covered with sharp bumps, and deep hollows, you have never seen a thin zebra. He is as fat as lard, but always hungry.

Kirui and Kipkelat

A Nandi raiding party set out from Kibos to make themselves rich on other men's cows. There were twelve of them, fine, ebony-hard men, with fierce eyes under the nodding ostrich plumes, and carrying tall black spears.

And one more, named Kirui.

Kirui was fourteen, which made him a man in Kibos. His spear was somewhat too big for him, his simi bumped against his knees, and the ostrich plumes had a bad habit of slipping down over his eyes. Often he began off something he wanted to say in a voice perhaps six notes higher than was becoming in a warrior. And, if he remembered, he coughed, and brought it down. It was his first raid.

They went down from Kibos to Kipkebus; from Kipkebus to Kapsabet, winding through the forest; from Kapsabet to Kholera, down the hillsides with the tall grass whispering in the wind; from Kholera to Mumias, between rocks as big as churches.

'Wait for me,' piped Kirui, and the last but one in the line of striding men growled back:

'You asked to come. Now keep up.'

They had seen no cows to take, or men to take them from, so they stopped for the night, ate cold corn cake, and curled asleep in the grass like cats.

'And about time too,' sighed Kirui as he wrapped a cow-skin round him. 'Eh, my feet!'

They woke at dawn, shook off the dew, and sat in a circle like wet, shining rocks in the grass.

'There's nothing here,' said the leader. 'We'll go east. Agreed?'

'Agreed,' said the rest.

'Well, that's settled. Then we march. But first, pass the snuff, Kipsaina.'

Kipsaina untied from his waist a little gourd of snuff, shook a pinch of black powder into the palm of his hand, and snuffed this greedily. He passed the gourd to the next man, and so it travelled round the circle until it reached Kirui.

'A . . . a . . . a . . . TISHO!' said Kirui a moment later.

'Quiet!' they snarled at him. 'Must you tell the world we're here?'

'No,' said Kirui in a muffled voice. 'No, I don't want to do that.'

So they went east, from Mumias to Yala, the rain from the lake now on their right cheeks; from Yala to Chemilil, out of the rain into the hot, dry thorn-country, with the sun like a blow on their backs; until they stood at the top of the great cliffs that overlook Miwani. Here they paused for breath, and listened, and, up-wind, they heard the distant lowing of cattle.

'Now, that's more like it,' said the leader. 'Close up there, and follow me.'

So when Kirui, panting up the slope behind, reached the top, they were disappearing among the scrubby, flat-topped trees.

'Wait!' cried Kirui, 'I've got a thorn in my foot. Please wait until I've got it out!'

'Stay there. We'll come back,' shouted the last man, but from that distance all that Kirui heard was a faint voice saying something. Then they were gone, and he was alone.

Kirui put down his spear and sat to attend to the thorn.

'Eh!' he gasped, 'but it's a big one. Oh! And deeper than I thought. Now, which way does it lie . . . Ah, I see . . . Eeee! Come out, you brute. Got it. And, now, which way did they go?' said Kirui.

He wandered for the rest of that day among the thorn trees, trying to follow his companions' trail. For a while he thought that bent grasses pointed the way; but then they spread, and divided, and he was unsure whether they had been broken by rain, or wind, or wandering buck. Then the ground grew bare and stony, and he could see no signs at all. But he went on hopefully. Until nightfall, when he knew he was lost.

He spent that night upon some dry leaves which had drifted into the bottom of a hollow tree, and he ate the last of his corn cake. In the darkness outside the tree things rustled and scratched and whimpered. Once, something larger laid back its ears, strained a great head up, and howled full-throatedly at the stars. Or so it seemed to Kirui. He did not do a great deal of sleeping.

The next day he wandered on, he no longer cared in which direction. The country was wild and empty, a place of deep, narrow valleys, and steep hillsides. At midday, on one of the greatest of these, he saw what he took to be grazing sheep dotted among the grass. But when he reached the place he found they were dry white bones, scattered on the ground. They had been picked very clean.

Kurui inspected them, and turned one over with his spear. Then he straightened up and looked round.

'I wonder what did the picking?' he said. 'There's something here that I don't completely understand. Or like.'

Leaving the bones he went steadily up the hill. It was a bare, wind-swept place, littered with stranded grey rocks, and from the top he could see for miles. The land spread beneath him, much as it must do for a hawk quartering its hunting ground. Kirui stared, and then his heart leaped. Down there, across a dozen little steep and tangled valleys, wound a great river. And beyond were blue, forested hills. Was it? Yes. That was the Yala River, and, beyond, the Nandi Hills, He knew where he was.

Tiredness gone, he gave a little leap of relief, and then ran singing down the ravine below, leaping from side to side of the tiny stream that chattered along its bottom, running between fern-hung walls of rock. He was going home.

Then something hummed like a harp-string, grasped him by one leg, and swung him up, and up, and stopped, leaving him dangling for all the world like a hare in a snare. And if a snare can be a looped, ten-foot cable of elephant hide, and the stake that held it the trimmed trunk of a morabe tree, then that is what had caught Kirui.

And while he gently swung high in the air the giant Kipkelat came out chuckling from behind the rock where he had been waiting.

'Heh!' he rumbled, wiping tears of laughter from his eyes. 'Haven't seen anything so funny for many a day. Bit of a skip, bit of a jump, and . . . wheeh! G O T him.'

Kipkelat was one of a race of giants who have voices deep beyond human knowledge.

'Now, come out of that,' he went on to himself. 'Careful. Ah! So you've got teeth, have you? No, it's not teeth, neither. Well, I do declare, it's a little simi. Let's have a better look at you. As I thought, We don't often get one of you, but you're always welcome. As nice a boy as I've seen. A thought skinny, perhaps, but that'll mend. Now, where's that simi gone? Simi! He, he! More like a needle. Eh! But it's as sharp as a needle too. We'll take it home. Might find a use for it. And for you too; eh, my little pigeon?'

And so, off they set, Kirui slung over the giant's shoulder, bumping against his broad slab of a back, and staring down at those ponderous legs devouring the miles.

Kipkelat lived in a great cave under one wall of a gorge of the Yala River. He owned three hundred head of cattle which grazed the rich grass of the narrow water-meadows both sides of the river. Indoors, he kept a parrot, a pet of which he was extremely fond. The floor of the cave was as wide as a field, and in the hard sand of this, Kipkelat drove a stake with two great blows of his club. Tunk! Tunk! And the thing was done. Deep in, and firm as if it grew there. To this he tethered Kirui with a thong of green hide, tossed the simi on to a ledge of rock near the fireplace, and went out to do his milking.

Kirui stared round. Outside, the river brawled, but inside all was quiet, and cold, and dim. In a crack running across one great rock wall the giant had wedged a bough as a perch for his pet, and on this the parrot stood, and inspected Kirui with mad, yellow eyes. Then it swung upside-down, and screamed. Kirui jumped, and the echoes ran back into the depths of the rock, until there was silence once again.

Presently Kipkelat returned with an enormous gourd of milk. He made a fire, vanished round a corner of rock, and returned with a vast collop of meat; the whole side of a buffalo, nothing less. This he speared on an iron spike, and roasted, turning all carefully so that the fat ran spitting into the fire. When it was done, he tore off a piece as big as a pumpkin, poured out a crock of milk, and gave both to Kirui, who cowered away to the extreme end of his tether.

'Eat up, my pigeon,' said the giant. 'We've got to put a bit of flesh on you.'

He looked at Kirui narrowly. 'About ten days' time. That's when I judge you'll be ready, and I'm one with a lot of experience. Now, eat hearty, and don't waste my time.'

Then he gathered his own enormous portion of meat, and retired to the shadows deep in the cave, where Kirui could hear him gnawing bones, and sighing with pleasure.

For five days Kirui was tethered there. The first day he ate nothing, only drank a little milk. When the giant found the food untouched he shouted in a voice of thunder, 'Eat! Eat!', and Kirui trembled. Then he felt himself weak with hunger, and ate what was given him almost without thinking; and Kipkelat was pleased.

The second night he worried with teeth and nails at the thong which held him. He found the hide too tough to break, and the knots too tight and cunningly made to untie.

Then he despaired, and ate and slept the days away. When he was awake he watched the parrot with dull eyes, and sat listlessly when Kipkelat brought his food and pinched him.

'You're doing better than I hoped,' said the giant. 'Eat hearty, my pigeon.'

And indeed, despite his fear and grief, Kirui, gorged and idle at the end of his leash, grew plump and sleek.

Now here something should be explained about Kipkelat, and it is this. He was, beyond doubt, a terrible creature, strong as an elephant, and tall as a tree, but, like most great folk, he had a weakness. Kipkelat's weakness was his right heel. Club him across the head, and he scratched at the place, puzzled as to what had tickled him; thrust a spear in his middle, and he giggled and told you to stop. But touch his heel with nothing more than a feather, and he rolled on the ground roaring with pain.

And there is one other thing that must be said: Kipkelat was lonely. Furthermore, like all lonely folk, whether giants or not, he talked to himself. When alone he often chanted a rhyme. It pleased him because it was his own invention, and went like this.

The heel, right heel; just strike at that.
It's the only way to kill Kipkelat.

He was, as you will have noticed, far from being a talented poet.

Each day, Kipkelat hunted, returning at evening with anything he had killed; and for long, empty hours Kirui sat on the sand with his thoughts, and stared in despair at the parrot. One day, from simple boredom, he spoke to it.

'Hello, bird,' he said.

'Hello,' replied the parrot, using Kirui's voice.

Kirui's hair rose. Birds that talk! He had never seen a parrot before.

When he recovered from his surprise he said, 'Hello,' a dozen more times. Sometimes the parrot answered, more often not.

Evidently a bird of moods.

Kirui tried something different. 'How do I get out of here?' he asked.

'How, how, how, how . . .' gabbled the parrot rapidly.

'How, indeed?' sighed Kirui sadly.

And then the parrot muttered evilly, turned upside-down on its perch, and screamed in Kipkelat's voice:

'The heel, right heel; just strike at that.
It's the only way to kill Kipkelat.'

There was a long silence, and then Kirui said softly, 'Thank you, bird. I will. If I can.'

That night the giant returned, cooked the usual mountainous meal, gave Kirui his share, and retired with his own to the back of the cave. Returning with hunger satisfied, he found Kirui's food untouched.

'Eat! Eat!' he shouted.

'I can't,' said Kirui.

'Can't?'

'No,' said Kirui. 'I'm too cold. It's so far from the fire here. If only I could sit beside that for a while, and warm myself; then I think I might eat.'

'Hm,' replied the giant, and eyed him shrewdly. 'Well, I don't see any harm in it. I'll lengthen the tether for a while. But mind, no tricks.'

He went to the stake, untied the knots easily with his great fingers, and paid out enough of the thong for Kirui to carry his food to the fire. Kipkelat retied the knots, and tested them carefully. Satisfied that all was safe he watched Kirui eating for a moment, and then went back into the depths of the cave. Once he was gone, Kirui reached up the wall, and took his simi from the rock ledge where the giant had tossed it.

He was sawing frantically with this at his tether when Kipkelat returned and saw what he was doing. Kirui stopped (the hide was barely frayed), leaped to his feet, put his back against the wall, and brought his simi up.

'Come within reach, and I'll split you in half,' he shouted.

The giant first stared, then guffawed.

'You? What are you? A morsel. A mouse. A flea. And what will you do this with, may I ask? With that needle you carry? Here, let's make an end to this. I've pampered you long enough.'

And the cave floor shuddered beneath his tread as he came grabbing.

Then Kirui, simi ready, dodged beneath the clutching hands, ran between the tree-like legs, turned like a cat behind one monstrous heel, and cut deep. Kipkelat bawled once and tottered. Kirui, glaring up, saw him coming like an avalanche, and ran for his life from beneath. The rock around him lurched and settled, the parrot leaped from its perch and screamed.

And Kipkelat was dead.

It took the rest of the night to saw through the knots, but it was managed at last. Kirui went out into the dawn that he had not believed he would ever see again. Across the river, below the cliffs of the gorge. Kipkelat's cattle grazed contentedly on the sweet grass. Fine beasts, all of them. Kirui crossed the river, and, choosing with care, cut out a hundred cows (he could not manage more), and began driving them home.

There was a great stir when he reached this. And, as chance would have it, no sooner had he finished telling the tale than the twelve men he had gone raiding with returned empty-handed, and looking glum.

They stopped in their tracks, and gaped at Kirui's cows.

So he had to tell the story again.

'And I still think,' concluded Kirui, 'that you'd have done much better if you'd waited for me as I asked you to.'

Which may well have been true, but I do not think it made him popular with *some* people in Kibos.

Kakara the Giver

Long ago, one of the Lake Kingdoms was ruled by a king whose name was Uni. But his people rarely called him that. They called him King More, for the exact reason that whatever Uni had—cattle, fine carved ivory, beaded stools, and the bright cloth that came from distant Zinj—he wanted more. When Uni collected taxes, and the tribute was piled before him, he looked it over with a cold eye, and then said, 'That is indeed generous, and I thank you. Now, what more?'

When they protested that there could be no more he said, 'We'll hang someone to improve your memory.' And it was marvellous how suddenly the pile increased.

He was not loved, but he was not ignored either. You could no more forget Uni than you could the toothache.

The neighbouring kings also found he was not to be ignored. One border of his land was the Great Lake, with a cloud of inshore islands. From here Uni's boats sailed across the lake, loaded with ivory, rhino horn, tortoise-shell, and slaves. At Mwanza, on the southern shore, they traded these for the printed cotton, copper wire, beads, steel blades and rare glazed pots which made Uni rich. But inland his borders were the kingdoms of Bunyoro, Ankole, Mpororo and Toro. It seemed to Uni that, great as his country was, he could very well enlarge it. So he made war. The kingdom of Bunyoro, Ankole, Mpororo and Toro were in an uproar with marching men and glittering spears, burning villages and stolen cattle, and their kings most heartily wished that Uni was at the bottom of the lake. However, since King More would not go away, they tried to deal with him. Bunyoro and Mpororo sent armies, which Uni fought savagely, and with fair success. Ankole offered him a present of their famous cattle, which Uni welcomed— and asked for more. Toro sent him a wife.

Her name was Wanyana, and she was beautiful.

She was the third daughter of the sixteenth wife of the king of Toro, and, of course, a girl. So it is quite obvious that she was of no importance whatever. The king, a somewhat miserly man, mulled over in his mind a number of things that might make suitable presents for Uni, and rejected them all as too valuable to part with. Then somebody suggested his daughter.

'Which one?' asked the king suspiciously. 'Not Naku. I'm not yet parting with anyone who's as good at making plaintain stew as Naku. Besides, she's promised to Kadu of Bunyoro.'

'No, of course not,' they said. 'What about Wanyana?'

'Who's she?' asked the king. He could not remember ever having seen her.

After they had explained he said, 'The very person. Send her at once. But see she doesn't take too many things. Uni can provide her with what she needs. After all, he's marrying the girl.'

So after Wanyana and her mother had wept she gathered her modest store of clothes, beads and bangles, and, with an escort of warriors and a court elder, set out for Uni's country. She knew that she would never see Toro or her mother again. But, being as sensible as she was beautiful, and knowing she could only expect marriage in a distant land, she dried her tears, and began to wonder what Uni was like.

When she arrived, and the elder had explained his mission, Uni was pleased. He had many many wives but that was no reason why he should not have one more. Besides, the girl was beautiful. He accepted the present and returned a long message by way of the Toro elder (whose work was to memorise such things), which began:

'Uni thanks you. Your gift is precious to him. But even more precious is the thought that now he can regard you as a father. Uni eagerly awaits the other gifts which, it is well known, good fathers always give their sons . . .' And so on.

The king of Toro was not pleased. 'Gifts!' he growled.

'When I've time to attend properly to Uni I'll give him a length of rope tied to one of his own burning house beams.'

Uni had a good house built for Wanyana beside those of his other wives. It had deep yellow thatch, and around it a high fence of reeds. Outside this was a garden where she grew her yams, bananas and lily bulbs. What time Uni could spare from war and rapaciousness he spent with her, for she delighted him. She might have been happy, but she longed for her own people and Uni's other wives were jealous.

After some time she found a friend in Bakka the Diviner. Bakka was a Mtoro who long ago had left his own land and settled at Uni's court. He was valued for the advice he sold on when and how to plant, whom to marry, and how to overcome bad luck. He was respected for his wisdom which he gave free, and he was loved for his generosity. A good man. Wanyana first came to him with a gift of a goat, for advice upon how she should conduct herself in Uni's household. Since Bakka was her countryman, she returned to enjoy the relief of speaking her own language. Rapidly she came to love the gentle kindness of the old man, and something like the feelings of father and daughter grew between them.

After a year, deeply troubled, she came to him for help. For Wanyana knew that she was going to have a child.

With simpler folk, such as you and me, the coming of a child would seem an occasion for joy, not grief. But then we do not live at the court of a Lake Kingdom. If the child was a girl, all would be well, for daughters were harmless, even profitable. But a boy; that would be a different matter. It was well known that sons grew ambitious to be king, and dissatisfied subjects often lent them a hand. Also when Uni died a large number of sons would fight for the throne

and tear the kingdom to pieces. Uni had as many sons as
he could easily keep his eye on, and wanted no more.

Wanyana knew in her heart that this child would be
a son, and she wanted it to live. She told Bakka this, and
after he had thought deeply he told her what to do.

'You must pretend,' he said, 'that you are sick and wish
to see no one except me. I will bring medicine and a slave
girl to attend you. When the child is born, if it is a boy,
give it to this girl, and tell her to hide it wherever you think
best. And send her to tell me where this is.'

'It will be a son,' said Wanyana, but went home somewhat
comforted.

A month later she fell sick, and after Bakka had visited
her he announced that this illness was the kind that would
endanger anyone who came near. He sent a slave girl to
attend her, and, good doctor that he was, and protected by
his art, went to her compound daily. Fortunately Uni was
away at war with Ankole, and no one else cared enough
to ask questions. The slave girl, a mute, brought and cooked
Wanyana's food. And in due course one night the child was
born.

Uni had a new son, and Wanyana hoped he would never
know it.

She wrapped the child in a soft cotton cloth, and over
that a fine leopard-skin, placed it in the slave girl's arms,
and told her to leave it at the bottom of a potter's clay
pit. Then she must hurry to Bakka and say what she had
done.

The girl did as she had been told, and when, talking
with her fingers, she had given the tale to Bakka, the old
man nodded, took snuff to help him think, and in the
morning sent for the potter.

This man's name was Bulo, and he came before Bakka

wiping the clay off his hands, and curious as to why the diviner wanted him.

'Sit down, Bulo,' said Bakka, 'and drink a little of this beer.'

'Thank you, Wise One,' said Bulo. 'This is indeed an honour.'

Then, after sipping, he smacked his lips and added, 'Good beer. It would be a waste of time for an ignorant man, such as myself, to talk while he drinks it. I'll just listen. I can do that and drink.'

'I've heard,' said Bakka, 'that your pots, once justly famous, are not what they were. The clay crumbles and cracks. Or so I'm told.'

'If I'd known that,' said Bulo, 'I'd have been here this morning without being asked. And brought a good goat too, so that you could advise me how to change this bad luck which is spoiling my pots.'

'My advice will cost nothing,' said Bakka. 'What you must do is to go at once to your clay pit, and whatever you find there, take home and care for. Also, I think you had best tell your wife this. Her help may be needed.'

'A good woman,' said Bulo, 'although, perhaps, it isn't I who should say so. Unusual woman, too, because she doesn't talk much.'

'It will bring you good luck,' said Bakka. 'That I promise. If, that is, you keep all this just between we three.'

'Won't say a word,' said Bulo. 'And neither will my wife.'

'I'm delighted that you understand,' remarked Bakka.

'Understand! I understand nothing,' said the potter. 'I leave that to my betters, and value my health far too much to go round understanding things I'm not meant to. But I'll do as you say.'

And he did. He fetched his wife and they went to the

clay pit. In the bottom of this they saw something bundled in a leopard-skin. Bulo jumped into the pit, and handed the bundle up to his wife, and by the time he had clambered out, she had unwrapped the skin, and was staring silently at the child.

For a moment Bulo's courage failed him. 'We don't know whose child this is,' he said slowly, 'but it's possible to guess. This could be dangerous. It might be best to kill it and say we found it dead.'

Bulo's wife had a great sorrow—she had no children. Now, she clutched the baby, and turned on her husband fiercely.

'Never say it!' she hissed. 'We need know nothing. Let Bakka live with that secret. The child is ours.'

'Who am I to argue with a woman at bay over a child, and a diviner,' said Bulo humbly. 'We'll keep it.'

After consulting Bakka they named the boy Kakara, and no child could have been better cared for or loved. Wanyana soon found a way to meet the potter and his family. So Bulo, and his wife, Bakka the Diviner, and Wanyana, the king's wife, were bound by friendship, and, perhaps, knowledge. At this time they may have confided in each other, or maybe they left it unspoken, but understood. But these four were all close to Kakara while he was growing.

II

Kakara became strong and tall, a skilled dancer, a man who might make a notable warrior. He helped the potter at his trade, and passers-by would stop to admire his strength as he raised high a mass of wet clay for its first rough moulding. But as a young man his greatest pleasure was hunting. With spear and simi and a bag of food he would vanish for weeks into the hills and forests, returning with leopard- or rare antelope-skins, and meat for the household.

Now it was time for the feast of the new harvest, when the first millet beer of the year was brewed. A wild and joyful time when, after carefully doling out last year's grain for months, everyone saw the new crop ripe and ready in the fields. They ate and drank their fill, and afterwards young men and women danced all night. This year Kakara led the young men. Great fires turned night into day, the smoke caught in people's throats, the drums beat like blood pulsing, everyone sang and clapped; and the king watched.

Uni was an old man, but still formidable, and even more wicked. His eye rested on Kakara leaping and twisting, and something nagged in his mind.

'Who's that?' he asked, and someone who stood near told him:

'Kakara, the potter's son.'

'He reminds me strangely of someone,' said Uni, 'and it isn't the potter.'

And, overhearing this, Itogo, the king's eldest son, bitter with waiting for his father's place, also looked carefully at Kakara, and determined to inquire further.

Bakka, whose ear was everywhere, warned them. To Kakara he said, 'You must go or Uni will kill you. I have an idea where you might be safe for a while, but we'll leave that for the moment. Wanyana, my daughter, and Bulu, my friend; you must think deeply about what is best for you to do. Uni will inquire, and I don't know how much he will learn. He may nose out that his wife was ill while he was in Ankole. He will be told that you are all often together. He may put a foot in the sandal and find it fits. Kakara he will kill on bare suspicion, he wants no sons that he hasn't handled and tamed. The rest of you will die if he gets proof.'

Then Wanyana and Bulu's wife said together, 'I will go with my son.' And, when they heard what the other nab said, turned and smiled.

Bulu scratched his chin and said, 'I spupsoe there'll be clay where we're going. That's all I need to make a living. But what about you, Wise One?'

'I'm too old for new places,' replied Bakka. 'I don't think that the king will kill me, but if he does my curses will cling to him like burrs to a dog's coat. He'll never eat porridge again without seeing me at the bottom of the crock.'

They fled that night, first to the lake shore, and then by canoe to Bukasa, the outermost of the Sese Islands. It was not done an hour too soon, for that night Uni's household warriors were at the potter's door, and others searching for Wanyana. They burnt both houses and took Bakka to Uni.

'Where are they, Bakka?' asked Uni.

'Even if I knew and told you,' replied Bakka, 'it wouldn't be worth your while looking. You've no time left.'

'They always spoke of your wisdom, Bakka,' said the king. 'I think it's been exaggerated. I'll wait until to-morrow for your memory to improve. No longer.'

'Memory is a strange thing,' said Bakka. 'It comes and goes. Mine has gone, yours not yet come. But it will. You'll remember me, Uni.'

They took him away, and when they went for him at dawn the next day he was dead. Perhaps he took poison, but there are not many who believe that. Diviners die when they wish to, and Bakka had done his work and was tired. But Uni remembered Bakka. He saw him at the bottom of the crock, as the old man had promised, and could not eat for fear. He grew weak, and died within a month. So Itogo ruled in his place, and, if possible, most people found this a change for the worse.

Omukama was chief of Bukasa when Kakara and his party landed there.

'Or as much chief as any other man here,' he said with a grin. 'I tell them what should be done, and they do as they like.'

He was a short, bulky Samia fisherman, bow-legged from years of squatting in a boat.

'We don't want to know where you came from, or why,' he went on. 'You can take any land untouched by the hoe. We'll feed you until you reap your first crop, but not lavishly, and not a day longer. Plenty of fish in the lake if you're hungry. Oh, and if anyone comes looking for you, they reckon with our spears as well. Here we look after our own—in a kind of fashion, that is.'

They took a piece of empty shore land and built huts, using reeds for thatch as all the islanders did. Only open-walled shelters were needed, for the islands are hot, and rain comes only from fierce, wandering storms which are gone in an hour. And there were no thieves. The Sese Islanders were of all tribes, and no tribe; men running from every kind of crime or misfortune; the beaks and bones that the Lake Kingdoms did not want. If they wished to rob—and they regarded it as a profession, like any other—they went abroad to do so. At home they were somewhat hard on thieves.

The women broke small gardens for yams and pumpkins. Bulu found clay, and took to his trade, sending pots to the mainland markets for sale, and Kakara fished. Omukama was his teacher, for the Samia knew fish, boats and

the Great Lake as a man knows the face of his wife. And
Kakara was a good pupil.

He learned the banks where the fish fed, how to burn
the palm-oil flares that drew them at night, how to use
hook and gaff, and judge the bend of a spear in water.
Omukama taught him how to judge changing weather from
the flight of birds or colour of the lake, how to hold the
boat's bow into the wind during storm. Among the reeds
together, they outwaited the patient crocodile, and speared
it when it inched ashore.

Kakara learned the markets that roared along the mainland shore, and which bought their fish. Here mountainous
women swathed in yards of gaudy cloth fought like lions
half the day for a bargain. There, a cowrie, on or off the
price of a cat-fish, was the breath of life. Kakara became
known, and liked, in these places. And here he found a
wife.

One day he saw a heap of string beds for sale, and, tied
to the bed legs, two half-grown dogs. One was as black as a
moonless night before dawn, and the other the colour of
new thatch. When he stopped to admire, both flattened
their ears and snarled, and suddenly a hand seemed to
squeeze his heart, and he knew he must own them.

Both beds and dogs belonged to a young man named
Ntare. Kakara knew him, for they had met on the fishing
grounds and elsewhere. When approached for the dogs,
Ntare looked at him, thought deeply, smiled, and shook his
head.

'They're not for sale,' he said.

Kakara offered double and then three times his first
price. Ntare threw back his head and laughed.

'When love comes in the window, wisdom goes out of
the door,' he said. 'I'd let you go on for the pleasure of
D

seeing how big a fool you'd make of yourself, but pity stops me. They're not for sale.'

'Then I'll fight you for them,' roared Kakara.

Ntare's laughter rang through the market. Then he grew serious, and looked sly.

'Listen,' he said. 'I'll not sell, and I won't fight. I'll give you the dogs, but on one condition.'

Kakare became cautious.

'This both is and isn't a gift,' he said. 'Your hand is closed on something. Don't think me ungrateful, but I'd like to see it open before I shake it.'

'Good,' replied Ntare. 'Sense at last. I'd begun to doubt if my plan was wise. I'll give you the dogs if you accept my sister Njumaki as a wife. She's not another gift, you understand. One doesn't give one's blood, and if you think that I will fight you. I'm asking you to take her from kindness, because she loves you, and doesn't know how to say it.'

Wonderingly, Kakare searched his mind for an image of Njumaki, and after a moment found one. A quiet girl who had once brought him food when he had sheltered for the night in her brother's house. As he remembered it, she had appeared scarcely to notice him. It seemed to Kakara that marriage to Njumaki might be pleasant. And, of course, there were the dogs.

So she became his wife, and with her came kinship to a swarm of fisherfolk. He built a house for her on Bukasa beside those of his mother and foster mother, and, in time, loved her deeply.

The dogs he named Darkness and Thorn. They grew huge, savage, and brave; and clung like shadows to his heels. They lay in the bow of the boat when he fished; their black and yellow heads resting side by side upon a gunnel. With Njumaki, the great dogs, the rough friendliness of his new kinsmen, and the wide freedom of the lake, it seemed to Kakara that he had a good life. He was content.

III

Itogo had not forgotten Kakara but he was busy with the usual problems of a new reign. His brothers and half-brothers had to be followed to where they had fled, and either killed or driven from the country. Tribute must be collected from every corner of the land so that all should understand that the royal stool was not empty. Also his neighbours looked thoughtfully across the borders, and wondered if he would be easier than Uni. Bunyoro sent an army to find out, and discovered that, if anything, Itogo was better at keeping what he held than his father had been. The king of Bunyoro wished that he had left the job to someone else, and while he counted losses, Ankole, Toro and Mpororo sent sympathetic messages. They also, almost absent-mindedly, each stole a province from him. At once, things were normal, and since his neighbours were now busily at war, Itogo judged he had time for Kakara. He sent for a trusted elder.

'You are now governor of Sese,' he told this man. 'Go there and clean it. The place is a nest of robbers and worse. Besides, they contribute nothing to the upkeep of my household. Take what men you need and do two things.

'First, collect all the wealth you find, and leave no one in any doubt that I am also king of Sese.

'Secondly, on Bukasa you'll find a man named Kakara. He has the look of Uni, and may be a relative of mine. I want his head, and the heads of all his household.'

Then he smiled sweetly at the new governor of Sese, and added: 'If you find the first difficult, I might understand.

But fail with the second and if I were you I'd think twice before I returned to explain why.'

The islanders fought back both on land and water. The boats struggled together in the creeks, the spears stabbed and on one island after another the houses burned. Bukasa was the last invaded, but when those of its men who survived from battles on other islands, smelt the stink of burning thatch drifting across the water, they knew their turn was near. Ten boat-loads chose flight. They were the hardier souls, or those whose past crimes on the mainland left them no hope of a future under Itogo. Among them were Kakara and his household. The rest stayed, and paid tribute.

They pointed the boats south, heading clear across the lake for the Mwanza shore. On the fourth day they saw birds flying to roost, and, an hour later, land. It could not be Mwanza, that was a further three days' sailing at least. By evening they were close enough to see it was an island; not so great as the one they had left, but still large and with low hills. It looked fertile, with trees and tall grass. The place was unknown to Omukama, who led the fleet, but when the boats drew together to discuss what should be done, one of the men named it.

'Nabuyongo,' he said. 'I sheltered there once for three days during storms.'

'Are there people?'

The man spat. 'People! What would they do here, lost in the lake. Where would you sell fish or buy iron? Why, if you lost sight of it, you could miss it when you tried to go home.'

'True,' said Omukama. 'We'll spend the night there and go on tomorrow.'

'We'll live there,' said Kakara softly.

They stared at him.

'You heard it described,' said Omukama. 'It's true. We could plant and reap, and no doubt there are fish. We wouldn't go hungry, but we need more than that. Hoes and spears wear out, seed must be bought, the women need cloth. I'm not prepared yet to live like an animal.'

'We'll discuss it when I've seen more of the place,' said Kakara. 'I have a thought, and, if it's sound, then we need go short of nothing.'

That night, beside fires burning between the boats stranded on the sand, Kakara told them what was in his mind.

'Here,' he said, 'we lie midway between Mwanza and Itogo's coast. To the east Itogo's boats pass carrying everything we need to make us rich.'

'And you would have us take it?' asked Omukama thoughtfully.

'Yes. Here is a safe home. We've a fisherman's knowledge of boats and the lake; our spears, and, best of all, a most pressing reason to hate Itogo. He won't let us live. Then let's try to make life difficult for Itogo.'

'It will bring down on us more than Itogo,' said a fisherman. 'All the lake kings share the trade.'

'It will bring us every man who hates and fears the Lake Kingdoms,' replied Kakara.

'There is one more thing,' said Omukama. 'If we live your way then you must lead us. I do well enough settling arguments over fishing grounds, but this business needs more than that. It cries out for the potency and luck of Uni's blood.'

'Uni owes me something,' said Kakara. 'I'll take his authority. I'll lead.'

Next sailing season, in the steady easterly winds following the rain, Itogo's trading fleet made its slow way home. The boats were heavy with wealth, and wallowed low in the water. The men from Nabuyongo came out of the emptiness of the lake, and fell on them at dusk. They fought by the light of fishing flares, the greasy black smoke drifting across the waves, and the raiders took all the boats, and the goods bought with a year's tribute.

Two months later they did the same, only this time the haul was larger. The markets along the lake shore were heaped with Itogo's stolen wealth.

'Buy fine Zinj cotton!' screamed the market women. 'It's from You Know Who, and very cheap. But don't show it to Itogo.'

The king raved, and from Bukoba to Jinja the lake laughed at him. He sent a war fleet which scoured the central waters until its crew looked hungrily at the hide stitching on their own thwarts. They found nothing. His next cargo of fine ivory hugged the northern coast all the way, a full month's journey creeping round the coast to Mwanza. Its route was the talk of every market twenty days before it sailed, and Kakara stole every tusk just outside Mwanza Sound. Next day he exchanged them for Indian steel in Mwanza, and the blades were on sale as far as Sese before the survivors returned with their tale to Itogo.

And, as he said they would, men flocked to Kakara with their spears and boats. It was a quicker road to wealth than fishing. He became a legend, the tall man with Uni's face in the bows of a boat. On one side a savage black dog, a golden dog on the other; and, behind, the eager dipping paddles and ranked spears.

His men, and soon the whole lake, called him the Giver. For it was a strange thing, but as those who followed him grew rich, Kakara remained poor. He took his chieftain's share of the captured loot, and gave it with both hands to the villagers of Sese, and the mainland fishing hamlets. Omukama once saw him take a fine bull-skin cloak off his shoulders and wrap it round a child who asked for porridge. It was not simple goodness, those who knew him best often thought it not goodness at all, for there was an impishness to his giving. He would haggle for an hour in the market selling a fine copper bangle, and when the woman, defeated at her own art, offered a ripe price, and said with a sigh, 'By Gogo, that's my last word, and you've beggared me,' Kakara would laugh, thrust the bangle into her hands, and say, 'I give it to you.'

And walk off leaving her staring.

Wealth slipped like water through his fingers, leaving him so paupered that his boat's crew had to feed him out of pity.

'Why do you give to these people?' they asked furiously.

And Kakara would reply, 'It's theirs. My father wrung it from them, and Itogo does the same.'

They would protest, 'Then, for pity's sake, give less, Kakara.'

And he would answer, 'I don't *give* anything. To give, you must first want what you give. I don't want it.'

IV

One day Kakara camped with four boat crews on Bugala, for now he went openly about the inshore islands. All men would have died sooner than betray him; or died quickly by their neighbour's hands after betraying him. At nightfall three men were led before him.

'They came by boat from the mainland,' said the men who brought them. 'We have the boat and the crew, and we'll kill them all when you give the word. We'd have done so before without bothering you, but these insisted they must speak to you, so we humoured them.'

Kakara looked them over. One was old and frail, with grey hair, and a great hooked nose. Another was thickset, and stood with his legs widely set and firmly planted. A war leader, thought Kakara. The third was a tall young man dressed in a fine leopard-skin, and it seemed to Kakara that in this one he saw something of himself. He told them to sit down, and had beer brought. It was sour rough stuff, made from palm cabbage, and with a few fish scales floating in it from the hands of the wife who had done the brewing.

Kakara apologised for the quality of the stuff, and the man whom he thought of as a war captain drank deeply and said, 'I've tasted worse.'

'Perhaps round a campaign fire?' asked Kakara. 'If, that is, I judge you rightly.'

He looked carefully at his guests, and then said to them, 'I think it possible you would prefer your names not to appear in our conversation. I've no quarrel with that, but I must call you something. Let me think. I'll call you . . .' looking at the old man, '. . . Counsel. And you . . .' to the warrior, '. . . Experience, and you . . .' to the young man, '. . . Now, what shall be your name? Authority, perhaps?'

'You read men well,' said the old man, and then, turning to his companions, 'Shall I be our spokesman?'

The man in the leopard-skin replied, 'Yes, Uncle,' and the soldier grunted:

'One or other of you. I never was any good with my tongue.'

'Kakara,' said the old man, 'we've come to make an offer, and ask help. Men begin to say, and we believe it, that Itogo has ruled for long enough. Someone else should sit in his place. Only war can achieve this, and when war is planned the first thing for sensible men to do is to count heads. We've done so. The inland border clans will fight for us; the heartland clans for Itogo. It is very even. Like a man gambling with knuckle-bones, impossible to say how a throw would fall. Now, only fools stake their lives on a chance of this kind, so we looked further. There were still two left out of our count: the Lake Fishing clans, and the Islanders. If these were added to what we've got, we might win. But they won't follow an inland man. They say, "What's it to us who sits in Itogo's seat? Whether it's King Up or King Down, he still makes beggars of us." But they might follow Kakara.'

'They might,' agreed Kakara. 'But there are two things left out of your story. When King Up is King Down, who sits on the royal stool?'

'You called me Authority,' said the young man. 'My name is Ruhinda. I'm Itogo's eldest son.'

'Welcome, kinsman,' said Kakara. 'The other question. What's in this for me, and those who might fight with me?'

'We'll divide the kingdom,' answered Ruhinda. 'For you, the islands, and the mainland clans facing Sese. Men say that you believe they deserve better than their lot. Then rule them, and give them what they want.'

'A thought comes to me,' said Kakara. 'Suppose . . . only suppose, mind . . . that when we've won, I try and take the whole. I could be king. There's as much of Uni's blood in me as in you.'

'It had also crossed our minds,' said Ruhinda. 'When we've won we might settle the matter, either by war or by tossing those same knuckle-bones that my uncle mentioned.

Then Kakara grinned. 'I'll have Sese,' he said. 'When, that is, we're in a position to have anything. The rest? I give it to you.'

So there was war. Kakara's islanders chased the king's governor out of Sese, and then for a time the islands hummed with men busily repairing shields and honing spears sharp. Night and day, the smiths hammered new weapons, and the little boats crowded the strands opposite the mainland. Itogo, swearing that he would leave Sese a graveyard, marched towards the coast. But he had not gone far before a messenger came panting with news that the northern clans were out under his son Ruhinda. Then Itoga grew thoughtful, his anger, though quite as great, was cold now, and he weighed chances. He sent fast runners to the clans who still followed him, asking for more men, chose what seemed to him a likely battlefield, and waited.

The king's of Bunyore, Toro, Mpororo and Ankole, wondered if now was the time to make a meal of Itogo. And they might have done if it had not been for some news that Kakara let drift to them through their spies. The kings learned that if they interfered, and Kakara won, he would stop the lake trade with Zinj for all but himself. If he lost, then he would stop it for everyone. The kings considered this, licked their lips, and decided to wait.

Then Kakara crossed to the mainland with his army, joined Ruhinda, and together they marched upon Itogo. They found him at a place named Katonga, beside the marshes of that name, and there a great battle was fought.

This happened a great time ago. If one listens to the story-tellers describing Kakara at the battle of Katonga it would seem that he was as great as ten normal men. That he came down from the clouds, Darkness to one side, Thorn the other, and scattered Itogo's armies to the winds. Believe me, this is only something that comes from time and much telling. He was, as I have shown him here, a great warrior who fought valiantly out of his love for the men of Sese. He and Ruhinda won their battle, and Itogo fled south, and vanished into the land of Burundi.

Ruhinda kept his promise, and Kakara became governor of Sese.

'What tribute shall I send you?' Kakara asked the king.

Ruhinda considered, and then said, 'Send, each year, one basket of fish. But make sure that they're fresh.'

And this is done. Under Kakara's rule, and after, the Islanders lived free of tribute, except, once a year, for a basket of fish. And it is fresh. Only half a day passes between the time they are taken glittering from the lake, until the moment when the last sweating runner lifts the leaves that cover them, to show the king his tribute.

Their colours have not faded at all.

The Hawk and the Hen

I was talking to Mrs Bahaya beneath the big mango tree which the Bahaya's grandfather planted in the corner of their yard fifty years ago. All around us were busy hens, and I noticed one of them behave in a strange way. It made a strangled, complaining noise, and squatted close to the ground beneath a small bush. Then it ran out into the open, and began to scratch most earnestly in the hard-swept earth, looking up as it did so. I also looked up.

There, high, circling lazily in the brazen sky, was a hawk.

Then, remembering that I was supposed to be talking to Mrs Bahaya, I turned to her in some embarrassment, and found that she also had been watching the hen. She smiled and told me this story. It explained, very neatly, everything that I had seen.

Years ago, hawks and hens were friends. The hawks wore round their necks the most beautiful bangles, carved in ebony wood, and decorated with fine, red copper wire. Anyone seeing such a thing could not help but exclaim with admiration, and wish they also had one. And the hens did this often, for they, poor creatures, were plain, and had no bangles. It was a trial to them. Also, it meant that since the hawks were so elegantly dressed, they were invited to many wedding feasts, while the hens were usually forgotten, and not asked.

Now one day there was a wedding feast to which a hen was invited. She was delighted, and went and told her friend the hawk.

'Odd,' said Hawk. 'They haven't asked me.'

'No?' exclaimed Hen. 'There must be some mistake.'

'I suppose so,' said Hawk. 'Ah, well, it's a relief. One gets invited to so many. Really, there's scarcely a moment to call one's own.'

And then there came to Hen a wild hope.

'Hawk,' she said timidly. 'Since you aren't going, and since you don't mind (I wouldn't ask you otherwise), could you . . . would you . . . lend me your bangle for the feast?'

'My bangle?'

'Yes,' said Hen. 'I'd take great care of it.'

'Hm,' said Hawk, and considered, while Hen hopped up and down in an agony of anticipation.

'Very well,' said Hawk at last. 'But you *must* take great care of it. My beautiful bangle. I don't think our friendship could survive the loss of that.

So she took it off.

First, they found that it would not go over Hen's head, and she despaired. All her plans had come to nothing. But then Hawk, growing interested in dressing up her friend, suggested that she wear it round her leg. And when they tried this it slid over Hen's claws and fitted exactly. It looked most distinguished, and Hen did a turn or so across the yard, while Hawk eyed her critically. Most becoming. She would be an asset at any social gathering.

It was a wonderful feast, and Hen greatly enjoyed herself. No less than four people spoke flatteringly about her appearance, and the last to do so was very handsome. She had great hopes, and why not? It is well known that one wedding often leads to another. Perhaps the excitement led her to drink a little more than was wise.

Whatever the reason, when she was flying home (hens flew much more strongly in those days than they do now), she dropped the bangle. She flew down and searched . . . and searched. It could not be found.

It was some days later before she forced herself to confess to her friend what had happened. Hawk was furious. Their friendship was broken, and, worse, Hawk swore that in future she would feed on hens until the bangle was found.

And so, to this day, when Hen sees the hawk, she makes a strange complaining noise. She is mourning for their lost friendship. And when the hawk has gone she runs from hiding, and begins scratching earnestly for that lost bangle.

Or so Mrs Bahaya said.

The Honey Bird

It was a Bukusu forester who first told me about the Honey
Bird. The forester lived in the Kakamega Forest, and
his job was to mend the fences found plantations of young
trees, so that cattle could not damage them before they were
big enough to fend for themselves. One day he gave me

some honey beer, which is very good, thin and sweet, and somehow cool even on the hottest day. We talked about the beer, and then went on to honey, bees, and finally to a bird which he said would lead a man to a wild bees' nest. This last, I did not entirely believe.

Later I found this bird mentioned in *The Birds of East and Central Africa*. The book called it the Greater Honey Guide, and said this: 'It has developed a most remarkable habit of guiding human beings to the nests of wild bees.'

So the forester was right, and when we next met I said I was sorry that I had doubted him. He laughed. 'Why believe a book before you believe people?' he asked, and I had no reply to that.

'I can tell you something else about the Honey Bird,' he went on, 'and that is it can be a dangerous bird to deal with if you don't treat it fairly. Did your book tell you that?'

'No, it didn't,' I said. 'How is the Honey Bird dangerous?'

So he told me this story.

Ten years ago there lived on the edge of the Kakamega Forest a man named Chekuli. He was a great hulking ox of a man, but good-natured and gentle. Not perhaps what you would call a brain; nobody ever asked for wisdom, but when a job required strength, why, for miles around, they sent for Chekuli. Just for the pleasure of seeing him use it.

A cow stuck in a bog, for instance. 'Where's Chekuli?' And when he arrived they would say, 'We've tried digging, and tried everything. Nothing will do. She's stuck, and so are we.'

Chekuli would scratch his slab of a chin, and say in his slow way, 'Why don't you lift her?'

'Lift her! Who could lift her?' And they would wink at each other.

'Why, I could,' Chekuli would say, and he would wade into the mud and heave her out. A full-grown cow!

Strong? As strong as last year's beer.

Now, when his father died, Chekuli took the farm. It was a good one. Hard up against the forest for wood and building poles, fine hillside grazing, a valley bottom for the corn, and its stream for water. With it came a flock of dependants: three aunts, and an old man who made baskets. Nobody was quite sure what kind of a relative he was. These old bodies did a few jobs in and out of the house, but most of the time they sat in the sun, sucked their pipes, and gave Chekuli advice. Sometimes he followed it, sometimes not. He did not grudge them their living, did not even think about it. They were part of the place and had been there as long as he could remember.

Since Chekuli was now head of the household it was time for him to get married. Everyone gave him advice about this. His neighbour Bahoya had four daughters, all strong girls who could hoe from dawn until dark. Any one of these would make a fine wife. And there was the Khasahala girl down the valley. True, she squinted a little, but you should see the load of wood that she could carry on her head. Enough to keep the fire burning a month. One load! What was a squint weighed against a talent like that?

Chekuli would have none of them. His heart was set upon a girl he had seen in Kakamega when he was there selling a cow.

Her name was Bwisa, and she was pretty in a rather wiry fashion. Her parents had sent her to school in Nairobi for three whole years, and now, what with dresses, and shoes, and the gourds she said they should throw away and buy tin tea mugs instead, she was so educated that it almost drove them mad. They were glad to see her married to Chekuli and off their hands.

So, proudly, he brought his bride home, and she took one look at the place, sniffed, and then set about putting it right. In no time she had the old house pulled down, and a new one built of bricks, with a corrugated-iron roof. And she chased the chickens out of the back kitchen. The three aunts went to live with relations at Butere, and the old man who made baskets was put on piece-work: four baskets a day for selling in Vihiga Market, or else. She embroidered, and hung a text over the front door which said W E L C U M WIPE Y O U R FIT, and bought a painted enamel teapot.

Then she sat back and regarded what she had done with satisfaction. 'Well, that's a start, anyway,' she said. 'Really, how anyone could live the way they did!'

Now, all these changes cost a great deal of money, and the biscuit tin beneath the bed in which Chekuli kept his cash was almost empty. So Bwisa declared that they should all work harder, spend less, modernise the farm, and go in for something called cash economy. Chekuli hired a plough, and tried corn and groundnuts, and Bwisa kept hens in wire runs and sold the eggs. They did so well that Bwisa relaxed the rule about spending less and bought a Vono Spring Bed. Nothing like this had been seen in those parts before.

Nearby, in a glade just within the forest edge, there lived a neighbour, a solitary old man. He was spare and stringy-limbed, with a wrinkled face and grey pepper-corn hair. Not a modern person because he wore nothing but a blanket, always the same one, year in, year out, getting more and more ragged.

'Really,' said Bwisa, the first time she saw him, 'he's

not at all up to date.'

The people who live in this part of the world belong to the Abaluya tribe, but this man was one of the Old People, the Wadirobo. Usually, you only see a Dirobo by accident, for they live deep in the forests and are very shy and secret. But this old Dirobo, being the last of his kind thereabouts, had put one leg into the world of ordinary folk and was almost tame. He had a small garden in his glade where he grew yams and beans, but mostly he earned a living by collecting and selling wild honey.

And what honey! The finest, darkest honey that anyone ever dipped spoon in, smelling and tasting of the flowers the bees had fed on.

Now there was a little mystery about this when you thought about it (and Bwisa was the woman to think about it). How did the old Dirobo come by so much honey? Everyone blesses his luck when he finds a wild bees' nest. He takes the honey, and everyone in the house eats it until they feel sick, for the next few days. Perhaps it might happen once or twice a year, not more often. But this old man brought a great potful to market every week, where it sold well and earned him a great price. And he had been doing so for years, never missing. That does not happen by accident.

'Depend on it,' said Bwisa to her husband. 'He's got some secret.'

'Uh!' said Chekuli, because his mouth was full of porridge.

'He must be crawling with money ' she went on, 'though, heaven knows, to look at him, you wouldn't think so. What he wants with it I can't imagine. A backward person like that has no use for money.'

'Ah,' said Chekuli.

'We could do with some of it, though. We haven't finished paying for that bed yet.'

'Any more stew left?' asked Chekuli, and after she had passed the pot Bwisa sat in a preoccupied way, watching her husband fill his plate.

'I'm going to try and find out how he gets that honey,' said Bwisa.

'Uh!' said Chekuli, because his mouth was full of stew.

She found an excuse to visit the Dirobo's hut. He received her gravely, invited her in, and, after polishing it with a fold of his blanket, gave her the one stool he possessed to sit on. When she had discussed the wooden corn pestle she wanted made (the old man was a clever wood carver), she sat and talked of this and that, while her little greedy eyes inspected the hut, and took stock of everything it contained. That was little enough; it was the barest of places. There was the earth floor, the soot-blackened thatch above, three hearth-stones in a drift of dead ash, a pot or two, an axe, a knife, and two old bed-skins. Nothing else.

'Really,' thought Bwisa, 'such a thing as progress might not exist.'

There was something more in the hut, though. She had missed it because her eyes had been blinded by the glare from outside. Beside the door hung a cage of the most intricate wicker-work. On a perch inside this sat a bird.

It was a small, dull, brown and white creature, with a pink beak. Bwisa did not remember having seen one like it before, but then she was not greatly interested in birds. However, she was interested in this one. The neat cage, and its occupant, were the only unusual things in that bleak hut.

'What a pretty bird,' she said brightly.

The old man's shrewd eyes rested on her for a moment.

'When one is old, and alone, it's good to have something living in the house,' he said. 'It sings to me, and brings me . . .' He seemed to consider for a moment, and Bwisa shaped her mouth to supply him with a word that came to mind. '. . . luck,' said the old man firmly. It was not at all the word which was on the tip of Bwisa's tongue.

When she got home she described the house and all it contained to Chekuli, but he showed little interest.

'How much does he want for the pestle?' he asked. 'I really don't see what you want with a new pestle. There are two perfectly good ones about the place already.'

'It's an investment,' said Bwisa darkly.

'I thought you said it was a pestle you wanted,' said Chekuli in a surprised voice.

'Oh, good gracious, what a fool I've married,' said Bwisa.

But that night, when she was almost asleep, he suddenly nudged her.

'What do you want?' she asked crossly.

'That bird,' said Chekuli. 'From what you tell me, it might be a Honey Bird. Did it have a pink beak?'

'Yes,' said Bwisa breathlessly.

'That's a Honey Bird.'

'What about it? What do Honey Birds do?'

'They lead you to bees' nests,' said Chekuli with an immense yawn, and the next moment he was asleep.

'Ah!' said Bwisa.

The next morning she was full of an idea—a most foolish one, it seemed to Chekuli—that they should go and hide near the old Dirobo's hut and see if they could catch him using the Honey Bird. Chekuli was not at all anxious to do so, but Bwisa usually got her own way if she set her mind to it, and she did this time. They spent the whole morning lurking behind trees near the glade, and all they saw was the old man sleep the time away in the sun with his back against the wall of his hut. It made Bwisa furious that anyone could be so idle.

She let the matter drop for two days, but then she persuaded Chekuli to come and watch with her just once more. They were in their hiding place early in the morning, and had been there an hour watching the old man cook and eat his breakfast, and afterwards smoke a pipe. Then things became more interesting.

First, the old Dirobo fetched a great clay pot from the house and washed it clean. Then he brought out a length of hide thong, and the bird in its cage. He tied the thong round the bell neck of the pot, slung it over his shoulder, picked up the cage, and set off into the forest.

They followed him.

When he had gone about a mile he stopped and put down the cage and the pot. He stopped and parted the wicker bars of the cage, and the bird slipped out and hopped on to his wrist. Straightening up, the old man gently threw the bird into the air, and it flew and perched on a branch high above his head. It sat there drawing wing feathers through its bill. This done, it said, twice, 'Weet-eer! weet-eer!', and then, with a flash of white wings, it was gone. The Dirobo sat upon a fallen tree-trunk, drew an iron-stemmed pipe from his rags, lit it, and sat puffing contentedly.

Some time later the bird suddenly appeared again. It flew about his head, chattering excitedly, 'Ke ke ke ke ke ke ke ke ke . . .' The old man put away his pipe, stood and shouldered the pot again, took up the empty cage, and followed where the Honey Bird led.

A little later he stood before an old dying podo tree which had been riven by lightning. From a long narrow crack in its trunk a dark stain ran down the bark, and the bees went busily in and out. They watched him light a fire, damp it down with leaves, and cunningly fan the heavy rolling smoke into the nest. The roar of angry bees died down as they became stupefied, and then, reaching into the nest, he began to rifle it. He took no notice of stray bees still active, perhaps their stings had no effect upon his leathery, weather-beaten skin. But first he took a flat piece of bark, laid it on the ground, broke a honeycomb to pieces, and spread a meal for the bird. Then he filled his pot with the remainder of the dark, oozing, oily combs.

Chekuli and Bwisa crept quietly away. So this was the old man's secret.

'I wonder how one could get a Honey Bird,' said Bwisa. 'It would be worth a lot of money to us.'

'You don't often see them,' said Chekuli. 'And I've never heard of anyone keeping a tame one like he does. Like one keeps a dog.'

'Hm,' said Bwisa, and they walked on in silence.

After a while Chekuli said, 'There's something strange about Honey Birds which for the moment I just can't remember.'

But Bwisa was deep in thought.

'Expect it will come back to me sometime,' said Chekuli.

That evening Bwisa said suddenly to her husband, 'I don't think we should say anything to anyone about what we've seen today. We ought to keep it to ourselves.'

'Why?' asked Chekuli.

'No reason,' said Bwisa. 'Just trust me about this. I know best.'

'All right,' said Chekuli. 'What's for supper?'

And there, for a time, things rested. Chekuli was busy with the harvest, and what time Bwisa could spare from house tasks, she spent trying to teach the old basket-maker to make some wicker armchairs, just like some she had once seen in the house of a missionary. Until one evening, when they were both sitting outside the house in the last of the sun, the old Dirobo came into the yard and stood before them. His wrinkled face seemed calm, but his eyes contained something else, it might have been anger, or it might have been pain. He did not even greet them, but asked Chekuli abruptly, 'Where is my bird?'

Chekuli opened his mouth in astonishment, but Bwisa said quickly, 'What bird?' and then Chekuli remembered that he was not supposed to know about the Honey Bird, so he echoed his wife, and mumbled, 'What bird?'

'Oh,' said Bwisa brightly, 'the bird you keep in that nice wicker cage. Have you lost it?'

The old man looked at her stonily. Then he said, 'A thing can be lost or a thing can be stolen. It's not the same thing.'

Bwisa bridled. 'Are you saying I stole your bird?' she said indignantly. 'What would I want with it? I would have you know that I'm an educated woman, and not at all interested in anything so old-fashioned as birds.'

And Chekuli said slowly, 'Now look here, Grand-dad, you mustn't go round calling folk thieves . . .'

The Dirobo stopped him with the stillness of his gaze and a little lift of his hand.

'I don't think you would steal,' he said. 'I'm not so sure about the woman. I've been wronged, but I'm a man of the Old People, and we've always known that it's useless to struggle when a man of the tribes wrongs us. You swallow it, or go away.'

'What impudence!' said Bwisa, when he had left them.

The Old Dirobo did go away. Next day, when Chekuli went to the hut in the glade to have the matter out with him, there was nothing left but walls, and thatch, and cold hearth stones. And he never came back. In a week the ants were busy in the walls, monkeys had pulled off half the thatch, and the dug soil in the garden was greened over with tiny weeds. It is wonderful, and frightening, how quickly a place goes back when there is no one there to care for it. In a year there would be nothing.

It was also just a week later that Chekuli was looking for an old axe handle. He thought he might find one in a tumble-down hut which they used only to store odd things. In the hut he found Bwisa looking at a Honey Bird in a neat wicker cage.

'Now, it's no use you saying a lot of things you'll regret later,' she said before he could get his breath back. 'If I'd told you about it you'd have given the whole thing away. You never could keep a secret. That old savage would have seen it written all over your face.'

'That's the old man's Honey Bird,' Chekuli blurted out.

'Of course it's his bird. Did you think I was going to let him keep something like that? He'd no idea of the value of it. And never shared it with anyone. Selfish old wretch! All that money he must have made, and no idea how to use it.'

'But it's stealing,' said Chekuli.

'It's not stealing at all. It's putting things into the hands of people who know how to make proper use of them. It's progress.'

'Oh,' said Chekuli humbly. 'I didn't know.'

Chekuli never did quite follow Bwisa's reasoning about the rights of taking the Honey Bird. But he knew she was educated and he was not. Obviously she would not make a mistake about a matter like this. It was above his head, and he was prepared to accept what she told him.

They tried out the bird a few days later, covering the cage with a cloth until it was safely in the forest where they were unlikely to meet anyone who would ask questions. The bird did its work just as well with them as it had done with the old man. They returned with a great pot of honey, and sold it the next day to an Indian shopkeeper for twenty shillings. Bwisa began planning to buy a radio.

The next time Bwisa went after honey by herself, since Chekuli was busy shucking corn. It had proved to be so simple that she was quite sure she could manage alone. Chekuli helped her to carry the pot and cage to the end of the fields where a long reach of the forest began. He watched her walk along the reach until, just as she was near the end, the little odd fact about Honey Birds, which had been in the shadow of his mind for weeks, stepped out into the light.

'Got it,' he said to himself, and then called 'Bwisa!'

She stopped and turned round, a tiny figure against the immense wall of trees.

'What?' she called back, her voice thin with distance.

'I've remembered what it is you have to be careful about with Honey Birds!' he shouted.

'What?' she called again.

'After they've found the honey, you must give them some. We didn't do that last time!'

She gave a little impatient wave of her arm, and vanished into the forest.

'So that's all right,' said Chekuli, and went back to his shucking.

In the forest the leopard sleeps by day, stretched along a bough high above a game track. He lies in shadow, like a great jewel in sombre velvet. He hears, sees, and smells anything that moves, long before it reaches him. If it passes beneath, he drops, and kills swiftly.

With excited cries of 'Ke ke ke ke ke ke ke ke ke . . .' the Honey Bird led Bwisa along a game track.

That night Chekuli waited and waited, and then, since Bwisa had not come back, he ate a cold supper alone.

She still has not come back.